D0403090

Night of
CAKE & PUPPETS

Night of CAKE & PUPPETS

LAINI TAYLOR

Illustrated by JIM DI BARTOLO

LITTLE, BROWN AND COMPANY
New York Boston

Little, Brown and Company
Hachette Book Group
1290 Avenue of the Americas, New York, NY 10104
Visit us at LBYR.com

Text originally published in ebook by Little, Brown and Company in November 2013
First Hardcover Edition: September 2017

Little, Brown and Company is a division of Hachette Book Group, Inc.
The Little, Brown name and logo are trademarks of Hachette Book Group, Inc.

The publisher is not responsible for websites (or their content)
that are not owned by the publisher.

Peacock footprint quote paraphrased from "The Elimination Dance" by Michael Ondaatje

ISBNs: 978-0-316-43919-0 (hardcover), 978-0-316-51397-5 (int'l),
978-0-316-36985-5 (ebook)

Printed in the United States of America

LSC-C

10 9 8 7 6 5 4 3 2 1

This book is dedicated to kissing.

—Laini & Jim

CONTENTS

HER

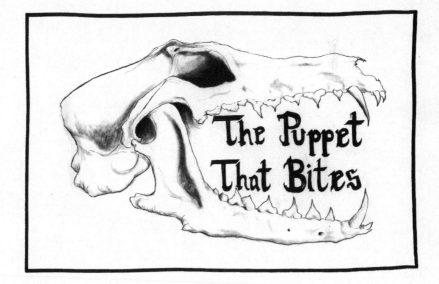

The Puppet
That Bites

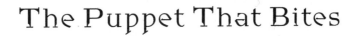

1

The Puppet That Bites

On top of the cabinet in the back of my father's workshop—which was my grandfather's workshop and will one day be mine, if I want it—there is a puppet. This is unsurprising, since it's a puppet workshop. But *this* puppet, alone of them all, is imprisoned in a glass case, and the thing that's driven me crazy my whole life is this: The case doesn't open. It was my job to dust it when I was little, and I can tell you for a certainty: It has no door, no keyhole, no hinges. It's a solid cube, and was constructed *around the puppet.*

To get the puppet out—or "let it out," in my grand-father's words—you'd have to break the glass.

This has been discouraged.

It's a nasty-looking little bastard, some kind of undead fox thing in Cossack garb—fur hat, leather boots. Its head is a real fox skull, plain yellowed bone, unadorned except for the eyes in its sockets, which are black glass set in leather eyelids, too realistic for comfort. Its teeth are sharpened to little knifepoints, because whoever made it apparently didn't think fox teeth were . . . sharp enough.

"Sharp enough for what?" my best friend, Karou, wanted to know, the first time I brought her home to Český Krumlov with me.

"What do you think?" I replied with a creepy smile. It was Christmas Eve. We were fifteen, the power was out due to a storm, and my brother, Tomas, and I had led her out to the workshop with only a candle for light. I admit it freely: We were trying to freak her out.

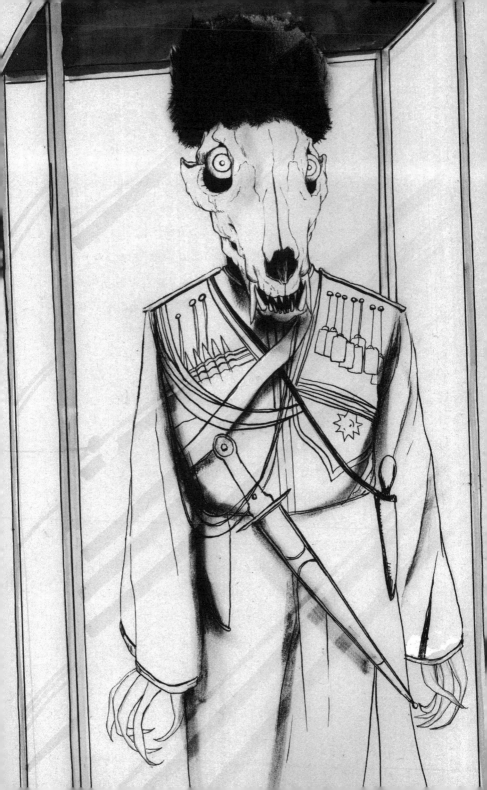

The joke was so going to be on us.

"Your grandfather didn't make it?" she asked, fascinated, putting her face right up to the glass to see the puppet better. It looked even more maniacal than usual by candlelight, with the flickering reflections in its black eyes making it seem to *contemplate* us.

"He swears not," said Tomas. "He says he caught it."

"Caught it," Karou repeated. "And where do grandfathers catch . . . undead fox Cossacks?"

"In Russia, of course."

"Of course."

It's Deda's best, most terrifying, and all-time most-requested bedtime story, and that's saying something, because Deda has *a lot* of stories, each one *absolutely true.* "If I'm lying, may a lightning bolt slice me in two!" he always declares, and no lightning bolt has yet obliged him, on top of which, for every story, he furnishes "proof." Newspaper clippings, artifacts, trinkets. When we were little, Tomas and I believed devoutly that Deda himself ran from the rampaging golem in 1586 (he has a lump of petrified clay in the rough shape of a toe), hunted the witch Baba Yaga across the taiga at the behest of Catherine the Great (who presented him an Order of

St. George medal for his troubles), and, yes, cornered a marauding undead fox Cossack in a Sevastopol cellar in the final days of the Crimean War. Proof of that escapade? Well, aside from the puppet itself, there's the scar tissue furling the knuckles of his left hand.

Because, yeah, that's the story. The puppet . . . *bites*.

"What do you mean, it *bites*?" asked Karou.

"When you put your hand in its mouth," I said, cool, "it bites."

"And *why* would you put your hand in its mouth?"

"Because it doesn't just bite." I dropped my voice to a whisper. "It also *talks*, but only if you let it taste your blood. You can ask it a question, and it will answer."

"Any question," said Tomas, also whispering. He's two years older than me, and hadn't shown this much interest in hanging around with me in more than a decade. It's *possible* it had something to do with my stunning new best friend, who he'd been following around like an assigned manservant. He said, "But only one question per person per lifetime, so it better be good."

"What did your grandfather ask it?" Karou wanted to know, which is exactly what we wanted her to ask.

"BABA YAGA"

golem toe?!

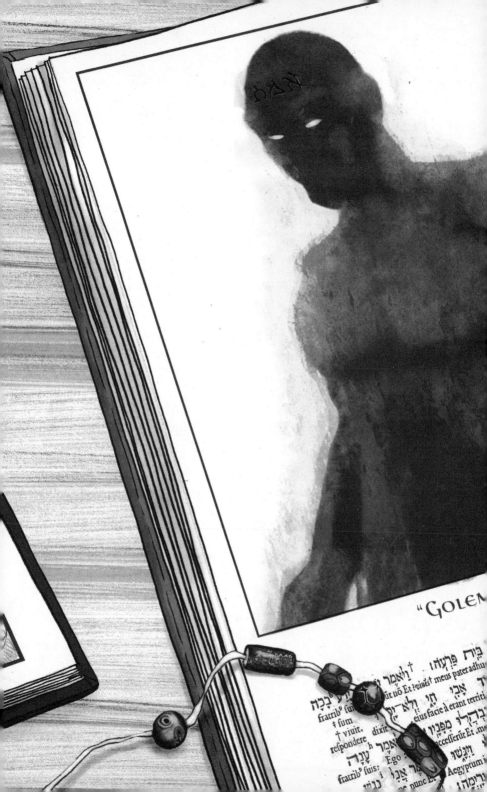

"Let me just put it this way: It's in the case for a reason."

The story is elaborate and gruesome. Truly, if I ever turn out to be a murderer or something, the newspapers can pretty much say, *She didn't have a chance to be normal. Her family twisted her from the day she was born.* Because what bedtime stories to tell little kids! They're full of corpses and devils and infestations, unnatural things hatching from your breakfast eggs, and the sounds of bones splintering. I thought everyone was like this, that every family had their secret haruspex uncles, their ventriloquist Resistance fighters, their biting puppets. A normal bedtime, Deda would conclude with something like, "And Baba Yaga has been hunting me ever since," and then cock his head to listen at the window. "That doesn't sound like *claws* on the roof, does it, Podivná? Well, it's probably just crows. Good night." And then

he'd kiss me and click out the light, leaving me to fall asleep to the imagined scrape of a child-eating witch scaling the roof.

And I wouldn't have it any other way. I mean, who would I be if I'd been raised on milquetoast bedtime stories and *not* forced to dust the glass prison of a psychotic undead fox Cossack? I shudder to think.

I might wear lace collars and laugh flower petals and pearls. People might try to *pat* me. I see them think it. My height triggers the puppy-kitten reflex—*Must touch*—and I've found that since you can't electrify yourself like a fence, the next best thing is to have murderer's eyes.

The point is, I wouldn't be "rabid fairy," which is Karou's nickname for me, or "Podivná," either, which is Deda's. It's for *mucholapka podivná*, or Venus flytrap, in honor of my "quiet bloodthirst" and "patient cunning" in my lifelong war with Tomas.

Anyone with an older brother can tell you: Cunning is required. Even if you're not miniature like me—four foot eleven in a good mood, as little as four foot *eight* when in despair, which is way too often lately—morphology is on the side of brothers. They're bigger. Their fists are heavier. Physically, we don't stand a chance. Hence the evolution of "little-sister brain."

Artful, conniving, pitiless. No doubt about it, being a little sister—emphasis on *little*—has been formative, though I take pride in knowing that Tomas is more scarred by years of tangling with *me* than vice versa. But more than anyone or anything else, it's Deda who is responsible for the landscape of my mind, the mood and scenery, the spires and shadows. When I think about kids (which isn't often, except to wish them elsewhere and stop just short of deploying them hence with my foot), the main reason I would consider . . . *begetting* any (in a theoretical sense, in the far-distant future) is so that I can practice upon small, developing brains the same degree of mind-molding my grandfather has practiced on us.

I want to terrify little kids, too! I want to build spires in their minds and dance shadows through like marionettes, chased by whispers and hints of the unspeakable.

I want to torture future generations with the Puppet That Bites.

"He asked it how and when he was going to die," I told Karou.

"And what did it say?" She seemed freaked out, which maybe I should have questioned, because though we'd only been friends for a few months and I knew next to nothing about her, it was clear she was a cool cucumber. The puppet's a pretty horrible specimen, though, and the storm was loud, the candlelight pale.

The stage was set.

"It opened its bare-bone jaws," I said, mustering my full theatricality, "and in a voice like dead leaves blowing down an empty street, it told him, though it had no way of knowing his name, *You will die, Karel Novak . . . WHEN I KILL YOU!*"

At that moment, Tomas bumped the glass case so that the puppet seemed to jump, and Karou gasped, and then laughed and punched him in the arm.

"You two are terrible," she said, and that should have been the end of it. That was the extent of our prank—amateur hour, I see that now—but . . . Karou gasped again. She grabbed my arm. "Did you see that?"

"See what?"

"I swear it just moved."

And she looked *scared*. Her breathing went shallow, and she was holding my arm really tight, just staring at the puppet. Tomas and I shared an amused look. "Karou," I said, "it didn't move—"

. "It did. I saw it. Maybe it's trying to tell us something. Jesus, it's probably *starving*. How long has it been in there, anyway? Don't you guys ever feed it?"

And the look Tomas and I shared then was more of the *um, what?* variety, because until that moment, Karou had seemed normal enough. Okay, fine. Karou never seemed *normal*, with her blue hair and tattoos and drawing monsters all the time, but she did seem mentally sound. But when she started worrying about the skull puppet being *hungry*, you had to wonder.

"Karou—" I started to say.

She cut me off. "Wait. It wants to tell us something. I can feel it." She was staring at it, and she hesitantly leaned toward it so her face was a foot or so from the glass, and then asked it, in this tentative, gentle voice—like you would a body you found lying in the street and didn't know if it was drunk or dead—"Are you . . . okay?"

For a second, nothing happened. Of course nothing happened. It was a puppet in a glass case. No one was touching it. Without a doubt, *no one was touching it.* Karou was clinging to me, Tomas had stepped back from the cabinet, and I know *I* didn't do it.

So when all of a sudden it turned its head and snapped its jaws at us, I *screamed*.

Tomas did, too, and so did Karou. Knowing what I know now, I laud her evil chops for that scream. Not for a second did it occur to me that *she* might be responsible. I mean, why would it? She clearly hadn't touched it. All my childhood terror over the Puppet That Bites came flooding instantly back. *It was true, it was all freaking true, and if that story was true, maybe all of Deda's stories were, and oh my god, how many times had I considered breaking the glass, and if I had, would we all be* dead?

I don't even remember running. Just, the next thing I knew, the three of us had crossed the courtyard from the workshop and were slamming through the back door into the kitchen, shrieking. The house was full of a Christmas crowd of aunts and uncles and cousins and neighbors, all well-acquainted with Deda's stories, and there were gales of laughter to see us—teenagers!—beside ourselves with terror, babbling that the puppet was *alive*. "No, really, it turned its head. It snapped its jaws!"

No one believed us, and Tomas sealed our fate when, within minutes, he backpedaled and claimed credit for the whole thing. "You should have seen your faces," he said to Karou and me, as if he could erase his own high, thin shriek from our minds. He put on that smug *oh you kids* face that is so deeply infuriating in older siblings, made all the worse because he was so absolutely *lying*.

For this treachery he would pay dearly a couple of days later, but that's another story.

The point of *this* story is that I will never forget the sound of those sharpened fox teeth snapping together, three times in rapid succession, and I will never forget the perfect clarity of terror that thrilled through me as, in an instant, my long-dead belief in magic flared back to life.

It wouldn't last. It would die back down again to a low flicker of uncertainty, but it turns out I was right to believe. It *was* magic. Just not the kind I thought.

The Puppet That Bites is just a puppet, but . . . Karou is not just a girl.

That Christmas Eve was my first exposure to scuppies, though I wouldn't know it for more than two years—*two years* she let me believe the puppet was hungry, that minx—until a couple of weeks ago, when Kishmish flew on fire into her window and died in her hands.

That was . . . a shock. Seeing Kishmish die was a shock. Seeing him *at all* was a shock, and finding out that he's real—or he *was* real—and not just some flight of fancy from Karou's imagination. At a glance he just looked like a crow, but once you focused on him, your brain started to issue error messages: Something wasn't right, wasn't normal. And then: Oh, it was his wings. They were *bat* wings. And his tongue. It was a *serpent's* tongue. Interesting, that, and it was just the point of entry.

It wasn't only Kishmish. Everything in Karou's sketchbooks was real, and the African trade beads she always wears are actually *wishes*. "Nearly useless wishes," that is, since scuppies are the weakest kind. She's traveling right now, trying to get her hands on more powerful ones, but before she left Prague she gave me a present. I'm looking at them right now.

In the palm of my hand, the size of pearls, no two alike in color or pattern and indistinguishable from African trade beads, are five scuppies. Nearly useless they may be, but even one scuppy would be more magic than I've ever held in my hand before, and I have five.

Five tiny secret weapons to add a spice of magic to a certain plan I'm cooking up.

What plan, you ask?

The plan to finally—finally, *finally*—meet violin boy, and sweep him off his feet.

Me, sweep *him* off *his* feet? I know. The laws of the jungle and romance novels would have it the other way around, but I'm not going to wait one more second for that. Milquetoast girls raised on princess stories might sit tight and bat their eyelashes in desperate Morse code—*notice me, like me, please*—but I am not that girl. Well, to be honest, I've been that girl for three months now, and I've had enough. What's happened to me? When Karou talks about butterflies in the belly and invisible lines of energy and all that, I make fun of her for being a hopeless romantic, but DEAR GOD. Butterflies! Invisible lines of energy!

I get it.

I feel liquefied, like a cucumber forgotten in the crisper drawer, and I want to hold myself at arm's length and carry me to the trash. Who is this sack of slush masquerading as me? It's intolerable. If Karou can sally forth to track down the most awful people in the world and steal wishes from them, then I can meet a damned boy.

I am a rabid fairy. I am a carnivorous plant. I am Zuzana.

And violin boy's not going to know what hit him.

2

That Kind of Alien

Here's what I know:
1. His name is Mik.
2. He plays violin in the orchestra of
   the Marionette Theater of Prague.

If we're talking facts, that's it. That's all I've got. But we're not talking facts. We're talking whatever I feel like talking, so I will tell you that Mik is one of those people you can look at and totally imagine as a kid. You know how some people were absolutely never children, but just came from a catalog fully grown, while other people you don't even have to squint to imagine them charging down the stairs on Christmas morning in superhero pajamas? Mik's the latter. It's not that he's "boyish," though I guess he is a little—but only a little—it's just that there's something direct and real and electric and *pure* that hasn't been lost, the intense, undiluted emotion of childhood. Most people lose it. They get all tame and *cool*. You know how some people think *cool*

equals *bored*, and they act like they're alien scientists who drew the short straw and ended up assigned to observe this lowly species, humans, and they just lean against walls all the time, sighing and waiting to be called home to Zigborp-12, where all the fascinating geniuses are?

Yeah, well, Mik doesn't sigh or lean, and his eyes are fully open like something awesome might happen at any time and he doesn't want to miss it. If he's an alien, he's an alien from a gray planet without pizza or music, and *he freaking loves it here.*

So there's a non-fact about Mik. He's that kind of alien. You know, um, as gleaned from casual observation. From a distance. Over several months of ~~stalking~~ watching. (It's not stalking if you don't follow them home, right?)

He blushes when he plays the violin. That's kind of a fact, I guess. He's fair-skinned, with those pink cheeks that make him look like he's just come in from the cold, and he's really *soft*-looking. Nuzzle-able. He's not hairless or anything; he's got sideburns and a goatee. He's *a man*, but he's got, like, *cartoon princess skin.* Don't ever tell him I said that, even though I mean it in the best possible way. He's got *the manliest* cartoon princess skin.

He's probably twenty-one or twenty-two, and though he's not miniature like me, he's not too tall, either. Maybe five eight? To the naked eye, he's decent kissing height if I wear platforms, though of course a live test will be required before official certification of Kissing Compatibility can be issued.

It *will* be issued.

Soon.

Or I might implode.

Because let's just say that the kind of alien *I* am is the kind from a planet of lipless dinkmonkeys and drooling slugboys, where affection of the facial variety carries  a deep risk of grossness. By which I mean . . . I have not yet elected to bestow the grace of my saliva upon another human being. I have never . . . kissed anyone. No one knows this, not even Karou. It's a secret. My previous best friend suspected, and now she's at the bottom of a well. (Not really. She's in Poland. I had nothing to do with it.) Until now, kiss candidates have been, at best, untempting. There are boys you look at and want to touch with your mouth, and there are boys you look at and want to wear one of those surgical

masks everyone in China had during bird flu. There are a lot more bird-flu boys at large.

But Mik I want to touch with my mouth. His mouth, with my mouth. Maybe his neck, too.

But first things first: Make him aware I exist.

It's possible that he is already aware, if only in a "don't step on the small girl" kind of way. We work in the same theater on the weekends. We occasionally pass within reach of each other. Without reaching. His proximity does something weird and unprecedented to me. My heartbeat speeds up, I become unusually aware of my lips, like they've been *activated for duty*, and I flush.

A while back, for fun and evil, Karou and I used to practice our *you are my slave* come-hither eyes on backpacker boys in Old Town Square, and I have to say I got pretty good at it. You need to imagine you are sending little tractor beams with your eyes, drawing the boy irresistibly toward you. Or fishhooks: grosser, equally effective. It works; try it. You have to really visualize it, the beam going out from your eyes and locking onto theirs, seizing them, compelling them. Next thing you know they're coming over and the new challenge is getting rid of them. (We found that acting jumpy, with lots of furtive glances over our shoulders and saying in a super-heavy Czech accent, all mysterious and imploring, "I beg you, go now, for your own safety, please," generally does the trick.)

Once Karou met that toolbag Kaz, our backpacker-boy games came to an end, but that's okay. I had perfected my *you are my slave* eyes. I should be set. But around Mik, my powers desert me. Forget come-hither eyes; I lose basic motor function, like my brain focuses all neural activity on my *lips* and shifts into kiss preparedness mode way too early, to the detriment of things like speech, and walking.

So while I could do the normal thing and try talking to him—"Nice fiddling, handsome man" has been proposed—I don't trust my mouthparts not to betray me by either stuttering into silence or puckering up. Also, there are always people around in the theater, potential witnesses to humiliation, and that is unacceptable. No, I have to lure him out, like a will-o'-the-wisp, tease him deeper and deeper into the forest until he is lost and doomed. Without the forest or the doom— just the luring. Like a Venus flytrap that says *I am a delicious flower, come taste me* and then *snap!* Devour. Without the devouring.

Well, maybe a *little* devouring.

Here we go. I have scuppies in my pocket and lust in my heart.

Tonight's the night.

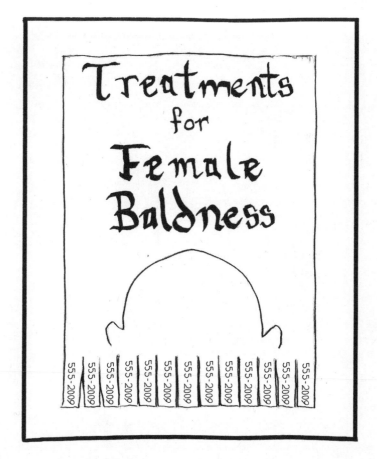

3

Treatments for
Female Baldness

I text Karou: **Tonight's the night.**

Her reply comes at once, which makes me feel like she's in town, just at her flat or at Poison or something, which she so isn't. She writes: **You will conquer. You are Napoleon. (Pre-Waterloo of course. And cuter.)**

Hmm. I text back: So you're saying I should . . . attack him?

Karou: Yes. Stun him with your amazingness. He will look back at his life up till now as the pale dream before the goddess. His real life starts TONIGHT.

A little over the top, maybe, but I appreciate the vote of confidence. Where are you, madwoman?

—South Africa. Trying to track down this poacher. Don't think he wants to be found.

—That sounds . . . safe?

—And fun! Someone stole my hairbrush out of my hotel room, and left a dead snake hanging from the doorknob. By its mouth.

—WHAT?

—Just another day in Africa. Better see a witch doctor for some all-purpose curse removal. Hope I don't have to drink blood this time.

—Blood? What kind of . . . Never mind. Don't tell me. DON'T.

—Human. Duh.

—I SAID.

—Just kidding. No blood-drinking. I better go. YOU.

Have a spectacular time falling in love tonight. Want to switch lives?

This gives me pause for a second, because it's the closest Karou has come to complaining since the night we stood in front of that doorway in Josefov and watched blue fire burn it to nothing. She was in shock, and in grief, and in *fury*, but never a hint of self-pity. After she spent just one day of reeling, hugging herself, and staring, we buried Kishmish in Letná Park, and then she kind of slapped the slackness out of her face and forced her eyes into focus and came up with a plan. Which in turn inspired me to come up with one, too, but yeah, mine's more kissing and less blood-drinking. So there's that.

I text back: If I say "no" am I a bad friend?

—Never. Just remember every detail. I need fairy tales right now. Rabid ones.

I love her. I write back: I promise. Please be safe. And that's the end of it, because she doesn't reply. I picture her disengaging a stretched snake mouth from a doorknob in order to get into a lonely hotel room somewhere in Africa and I feel this mix of disbelief

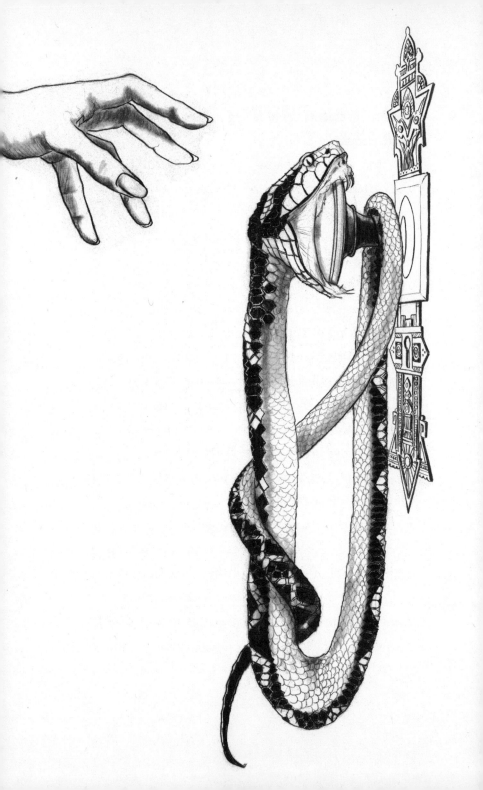

and belief, protectiveness and vicarious sadness, lost-ness. Guilt. Part of me thinks I should be with her on this crazy chase she's on, but I know I'm not fit for it. I can't fight, or speak Zulu or Urdu or whatever, and she'd have to worry about protecting me, and anyway, I did offer. She said no. She said I'm her anchor: I have to connect her to "real life," stay in school, keep her updated on Wiktor the living mummy, and Professor Anton's nose hair, and whether Kaz dares show his face at Poison Kitchen.

And Mik. I have to talk to Mik. She was pretty insistent about that.

If all goes well tonight, there *will* be talking. At some point. One assumes. I'm just not starting with it. I'm starting with a drawing. I've been working on it for a couple of weeks, redoing it over and over, and it's finally good enough: a drawing worthy of launching a love affair.

Love affair. Doesn't that sound so middle-aged? And also ill-fated. Like *ill-fated* is an understood pre-fix to *love affair*. Well, ill-fated is fine, as long as it's a *meaty and fraught* ill-fated love affair, not a pale and insipid one. I'm not looking for fate. I'm seventeen.

I'm looking for kissing, and to move forward a few paces on the game board. You know, do some Living.

(With my lips.)

The drawing's in my bag with my other . . . props. A few things have already been set up around town. It all had to be ready before I go to work, and I go to work . . . *now*.

Hello, Marionette Theater of Prague. Just another Saturday. Just walking up the steps with my bag of tricks, no scheming here . . .

Oh my god, there he is.

Knit cap, brown leather jacket, violin backpack. Sweet, cold-pinked cheeks. What a lovely display of personhood. He's like a good book cover that grabs your gaze. *Read me. I'm fun but smart. You won't be able to put me down.* There's a little bounce in his walk. It's music. He's got headphones on—the fat, serious kind, not the weenie earbud kind. I wonder what he's listening to. Probably Dvořák or something. He's wearing a pink tie. Why don't I hate it? I hate pink. Except on Mik's cheeks.

Hello, Mik's cheeks. Soon we shall know each other better.

Aah! Eye contact. Look away!

(Did he just . . . *blush*?)

Feet, help me out here. We're on a collision course. Unless we take immediate evasive action, we're going to meet him right at the door.

Panic!

Hey, look at this fascinating notice on the wall! I must pause here and tear off one of these little phone-number tabs so that I can call and inquire about the life-changing effects of . . .

Treatments for female baldness?

Awesome.

"It's not for me," I blurt, but the danger is past. While I was staring in rapt fascination at the female-baldness flyer, Mik slipped into the building.

Close call. We almost—in Karou parlance— "entered each other's magnetic fields for the first time." He would have had to hold the door for me. I would have had to acknowledge it with a nod, a smile, a *thank you*, and then walk in front of him down the entire length of the hallway, wondering whether he was looking at me. I know how that would go. I'd suddenly become conscious of the many muscle groups involved in the art of walking, and try to consciously control each of them like a puppeteer, and end up looking like I'm in a loaner body I haven't mastered yet.

This way, I can walk down the hallway looking at *him.*

Hello, back of Mik.

On his violin backpack is a bumper sticker that reads:

Which totally does not make me imagine Mik in the bath. Because that would be wrong.

Good-bye, back of Mik.

He goes through his doorway, and I go through mine, and thus is perpetuated for another night one of the world's great injustices: the segregation of musicians and puppeteers.

They have their backstage lounge, we have ours. You'd think someone's afraid we might rumble. *There's a cellist on our turf—get him!* Or, more likely but less interesting, it's a simple matter of space. Neither lounge is very big; they're just windowless rooms with lockers and a couple of sad couches. The musician couches are slightly sadder than ours, one clue to the hierarchy here. Puppeteers rule the roost, but it's not a very posh roost. In general, musicians respect their status (i.e., easily replaceable), but the singers, not so much.

The reason I hate it when we perform operas—like now, we're doing Gounod's *Faust*—isn't because I don't like opera. I am not a philistine. I just don't like opera *singers.* Especially sultry Italian sopranos in heavy eyeliner who go out for drinks with the strings section after the show. *Ahem*, Cinzia "fake beauty mark" Polombo.

Anyway. It's the puppeteers who matter around here. There are ten, six of whom are in the lounge ahead of me, pretty well filling it.

"Zuzana," Prochazka says the second he sees me. "Mephistopheles is drunk again. Would you mind?"

Drunken devil. All in a day's work. To be clear, I am not a puppeteer. I am a puppet-*maker*, a different animal altogether. Some puppeteers do both: build and perform. But my family has always stuck to fabrication, with the idea that you can be decent at two high art forms, or you can excel at one. We excel. Excellently. Still, it behooves a puppet-maker to understand puppeteering. My professor at the Lyceum—Prochazka, who

also happens to be lead puppeteer here—requires practical theatrical experience, so here I am. I scurry and fetch for the puppeteers, restring marionettes, retouch paint, mend costumes, and lend a spare pair of hands for easy things like fluttering birds or clip-clopping the horse hooves.

In this case, Mephistopheles has a loose string, making him list drunkenly to one side. It's an easy fix. "Sure," I say, and put my stuff in my locker, more mindful than usual of the contents of my bag. Once the lounges clear out—puppeteers to the stage and musicians to the orchestra pit—I have some sneaking to do. The thought of it kicks my heartbeat sideways.

I have to break into Mik's violin case.

I grab my tool kit. First I have a devil to sober up.

4

Drastic

I t's Act II. I can hear Mephistopheles singing. I text
Karou: Kindly confirm: If someone's evil, then killing
them isn't murder. It's SLAYING, and not only legal but
encouraged. Correct?

No reply.

After a minute, I text again: Taking your silence as

a YES. Sharpening knife. Text now to stop me. 3—2—1 . . .
Okay then. Here I go.

Still no reply.

One last text: It's done. Am currently dragging an
opera singer to the taxidermist by her hair. Plan to have

her stuffed and mounted above Aunt Nedda's TV.

For a moment, my frustration over the soprano is undercut by anxiety as I ponder what Karou might be doing in South Africa that she can't answer her phone. Poacher, or witch doctor? I have no success imagining either, and resume frustration.

ARGH! Prochazka kept me scurrying during Act I, then there were sets to change, and just when I was going to slip away, Hugo had to

pee and handed off Siebel to me, even though I am not cleared to operate a marionette in a show! I didn't have to do anything but make it stand around, at least, and when Hugo came back, I made my escape—back to the puppeteers' lounge to grab my drawing, and then . . . just as I was about to creep into the musicians' lounge . . .

"Excuse me. Girl!"

Cinzia Polombo appeared in the doorway. *Girl?* She actually snapped her fingers to get my attention. Oh yes. But it gets better. She handed me her empty coffee cup and, because she doesn't speak Czech, said in English, with a luxuriant and imperious *R* roll, "*Hurrry.*"

Oh. I hurried.

If anyone has ever filled a coffee cup with cigarette butts faster than I did tonight, I would be very much surprised.

"Is that not what you wanted?" I asked her in purest innocence when she gasped and looked aghast.

"Coffee! I want coffee!"

"*Ohhh.* Of course," I said. "That makes so much more sense. I'll be right back." And I was right back. I handed her the cup, now full of cigarette butts *and* coffee, and kept walking.

"*Disgraziata!*" she shrieked at me, dashing the contents to the floor, but I just kept going, back into the puppeteers' lounge, where I sit now on the sadder of two sad sofas, thwarted. Cinzia is still in the musicians' lounge, where she should not be. Her cue is any minute. What's she doing in there, aside from cursing in Italian? I'm going to lose my chance!

My phone vibrates. It's Karou. Finally. She texts: Go to the taxidermist on Ječná. They're the best with humans.

—Perfect. Thanks for the tip. Find that poacher?

—Much to his dismay.

—Wishes?

—A slot-machine jackpot of shings. Nothing stronger, though.

That sucks. She's looking for more powerful wishes, and shings, I know, are only a little better than scuppies. I text: Well, better than nothing?

—Yeah. So tired. Going to sleep now. GO FORTH AND CONQUER!

Again, whatever went down in South Africa, I can't begin to imagine it. As for the taxidermist, for a second I consider checking to see if there really is one on Ječná, but I dismiss the thought. If Karou was in the habit of having humans stuffed, that jackass *Kaz* would not still be walking around.

At the thought of Kaz, and to the continued sound track of a high-strung soprano cursing in Italian, I can't help but imagine what I might do in this moment with a limitless supply of scuppies. Really, Karou was incredibly restrained. *I* could not be trusted. I would be afflicting people with itches every second, at the slightest provocation. Think about it. With the power of itch—even better, the power of *cranny* itch—you'd be master of any situation.

Maybe not *any* situation. It wouldn't really help me with Mik.

Anyway. I'm not going to waste a single scuppy on Cinzia Polombo. I will preserve them for Mik-enchantment.

IF I EVER GET MY CHANCE TO INVADE HIS VIOLIN CASE, DAMN IT.

Finally: a door slam, and stomping, and Cinzia is out of the way. I take my drawing—it's rolled up like a scroll, edges burned, and tied with a black satin ribbon—and creep to the door of the musicians' lounge. It's ajar, and I can see that there's no one inside. No sense waiting. A flash and I am in, opening locker doors, mindful that if anyone were to walk in, I would absolutely look like a thief. I don't know which locker is Mik's, and it's impossible to open and close metal doors quietly, and some of them have locks on them, so I can only hope for the best. . . .

And then I find it. *Everything is a miracle. It is a miracle that one does not melt in one's bath.*

Everything is a miracle, is it? Ask me again at the end of the night.

I open the violin case and put the scroll inside. I close it, shut the locker, and back away. Time to escape. I flash back out the door, skirt Cinzia's coffee-and-cigarette splash, and slide back into the puppeteers' lounge, where I take a deep breath. Another. Another. Then I put on my coat, gather my things.

This is the moment when I walk away from the marionette theater, possibly forever. I feel like a brave Resistance worker who has just planted a bomb, and will now walk away, cinematically, without a backward glance. Because here's what I've decided: If things do not go well tonight, I am never coming back here. It's the only way I can do this, by removing the inevitability of embarrassment. I never have to see Mik again. There will be no awkwardness, no blushing.

No blushing.

I'm struck suddenly by the very real possibility of never seeing Mik blush again, and . . . my heart hurts. My heart has never hurt before. It's real pain, like a bad

bruise, and catches me off guard. I always thought people were making that up. It makes me wonder about
kissing and fireworks and all the other stuff I always
assumed was made up. And the pain comes again,
because this is it, things are set in motion, and soon
I'll know, one way or the other. He'll come or he won't.

What if he doesn't come?

Oh god. Is this too drastic? Maybe I should have just
had faith in the normal way: ferocious blushing, time
passing, hoping and pining, always alert for some sign
of interest until an exchange of small talk can occur.
("Have you tried this treatment for female baldness?
I hear it's life-changing.") And maybe over *more* time
small talk turns into shuffling toward shared coffee . . .
or maybe the blushing just goes on and on and nothing ever happens, drastic or otherwise, and then it's
like in a TV show when they string the sexual tension
between two characters out for too long and you stop
caring and it all just turns to dust?

No. I can't take dust, or small talk, or shuffling. It's
got to be drastic. One way or another, tonight I'll know.

I want to go backstage and peer into the orchestra pit one last time, but if I do, one of the puppeteers

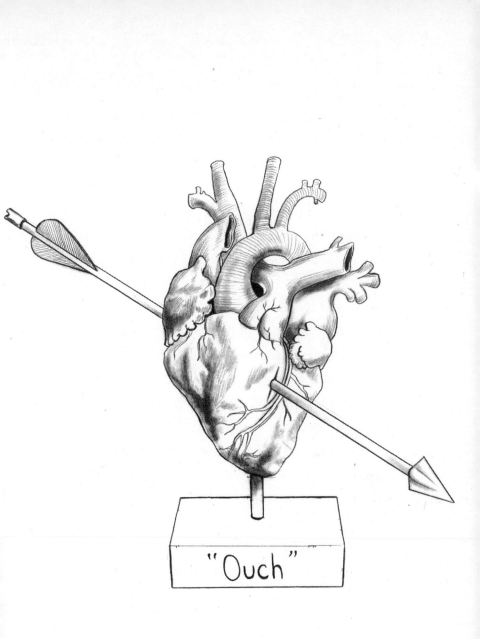

is sure to snag me for some job, and I won't be able to escape. Still, I pause at the stage door and listen. I hear Cinzia singing Marguerite, this tragic character debauched in a devil's bargain. She seems to have mastered her diva rage and actually sounds pretty good . . . for a third-rate soprano singing in a marionette theater, anyway . . . but that's not what I want to hear. I listen for the violin.

There it is, this sound that rises out of the music like a beam of light cutting through darkness. It's as sweet as love, so goddamn beautiful I could cry, and it's like my whole being forms the word *please*.

I don't believe in prayer, but I do believe in magic, and I want to believe in miracles.

Please come, I think through the wall, sending the words toward the sweet, pure sound, and the sweet, pure boy who's making it.

And then I leave.

It's snowing. I wrap my scarf around my face and feel a kind of peace. I've played my gambit.

It's up to him now.

HIM

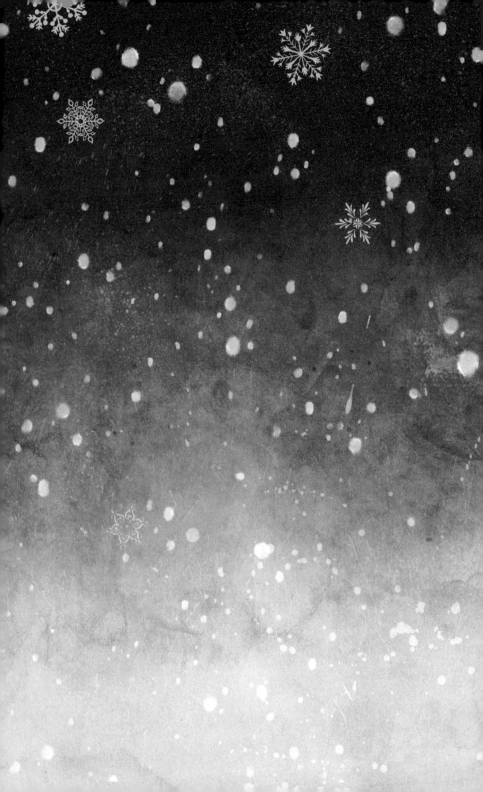

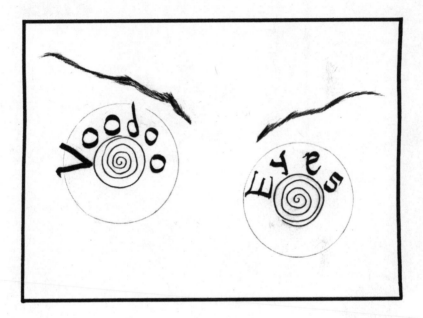

5

Voodoo Eyes

The curtain drops. The music dies away and applause overcomes it, and when I lower my violin, another Saturday night sits like a cat on a fence.

I'm not a fan of cats. With one shining exception. Wolfgang established an impossible standard, then died when I was ten, and every cat since has been a source of

disappointment. You hold out your hand to them, and they just look at it, and since they're not stupid, this act can only be interpreted as mockery.

Yeah, buddy, that's a hand. You've got two of those bad boys. Good for you.

Not: *Oh, you'd like to pet me? Let me come closer, because I like you, too.*

That's me and Saturday night lately. It just looks at my hand until, ashamed, I lower it and try to pretend I didn't really want to pet it anyway. The thing that I want to happen consistently does not happen. Mocked by fate? Maybe.

Maybe tonight will be different. It didn't begin well, but there's always hope.

"Party at Stooge's," says Radan as we file out of the orchestra pit, and that's the opposite of hope. It's the cat glaring at me, because it's where I'll probably end up tonight, and if I do, it will mean that for yet another Saturday, *she* will have slipped through my fingers. *She* will not be at Stooge's, would never be at Stooge's. I don't know where she goes after work, but I imagine stars and mist and halls of mirrors, and I want to be there, too.

I want to do mysterious and improbable things alongside a fierce and beautiful girl who looks like a doll brought to life by a sorcerer.

Is that really so much to ask?

I look for her in the hallway, but don't see her. And the door to the puppeteers' lounge is open, so I see as I pass that she's not in there, either. Did I already miss her? Probably.

Can't blame fate, I know that. It's my own suffocating idiocy. Why can't I just speak to her? I was going to earlier, when we were walking into the theater. It's embarrassing, but I'd waited under the awning across the street until I saw her coming. Only for a couple of minutes. Nothing weird. I don't know what I would have said, anyway. Probably something inane, like, "Looks like snow." Or possibly "I like cake." (She likes cake. This is one of four things I know about her. The others are: 2. Her name is Zuzana, 3. she's in her last year at the Lyceum, so is probably eighteen, which is young but not heinously young, and 4. she can freeze a person's blood with a look. I've seen it happen, though I have not been on the receiving end. She has voodoo eyes, and is more than slightly terrifying. Hence the not-yet-talking-to-her.) But I said nothing,

inane or otherwise, because she halted abruptly to consider a flyer on the wall, and I didn't know what to do but keep walking.

Damn it.

I wonder what the flyer was. I'll have to check on my way out. Not sure I want to, though. I'm afraid it will confirm my suspicion that she was just trying to avoid me.

The moment I walk into the musicians' lounge, a voice cries my name, and I cringe. "Mik!"

Cinzia. "*Meeek*," she pronounces it, and it sounds like a condemnation: *meek!* And then she's right in front of me and I shrink a little. I can't help it. Being looked at by Cinzia is what I imagine having a red dot painted on your forehead by a sniper rifle feels like. Tuck, duck, and roll.

"Did I sound not good tonight?" she asks in English, with an exaggerated expression of woe. Everything about Cinzia is exaggerated, from her eyeliner to the way she walks, every step hip-slamming an invisible bystander out of her way.

"What? Uh. You were fine." Just what every soprano longs to hear at the end of a show. *You were fine.*

"I was give a shock, is difficult to be calm, for singing."

I have no plans to ask the source of this shock, but she's already telling me. I'm at my locker, opening it, not really paying attention, when I hear the words *puppet girl* and tune abruptly in. "She did *what*?" I ask.

"I send her for coffee, she bring me cup full of cigarette butts. Can you believe?"

Actually, I can't. "You sent her for coffee?" This is the part I can't believe. Had Cinzia failed to notice the voodoo eyes? "She's not a coffee-girl. She's a puppet-maker."

Cinzia blinks. "No. The girl, the small one."

I nod. "Right. The small girl." Absurdly, I feel possessive talking about her. I think that this is the first time I ever *have* talked about her, and I have no wish to do so with Cinzia. "Anyway," I tell her, "we get our own coffee here."

She frowns at me. "She put cigarettes in my coffee," she says, like I've missed the point, and all I can do is try not to smile, because yeah, that's what you'd do to Cinzia if you were the kind of person who just did what you wanted. So I guess Zuzana is the kind of person who does what she wants? That doesn't exactly bode well for me, because wouldn't she have talked to me by now if she had any interest in me?

How pathetically passive, waiting for her to do the talking. That's not who I want to be. I want to be the guy in a movie who's, I don't know, out walking his rabbit on a leash (I don't have a rabbit) and knows exactly how to strike up a quirky, compelling conversation. Though maybe if you're walking a rabbit on a leash, you don't even have to speak; the rabbit does the work for you.

Not that Zuzana seems like the rabbity type. Maybe if I were walking a fox on a leash. Or a hyena. Yeah, if I had a hyena, I'd probably never have to start a conversation again.

Except for, "Sorry my hyena ate your leg."

I take my violin case out of my locker and open it, and . . . there's something in it. A scroll of some sort, with burned edges like a pirate's treasure map. Some gimmicky party invitation? I don't know. I guess I stare at it a second too long, because Cinzia follows my gaze, and what she says next changes the weight of the air.

"*She* had this!" she declares, in a tone of triumphant denouncement. "The small girl. *She* had this when I give her coffee cup."

What? Zuzana? My brain
turns slowly. How could . . .
something that Zuzana was
holding . . . end up in my violin
case?

Hope is tentative. The cat
does not approach, but it's possible that it's regarding
my outstretched hand with something like interest.

It's also possible it's all just a mistake.

Cinzia reaches for the scroll and, without thinking, I knock her hand away—lightly—and when I look
at her face, her nostrils are flared. She's giving me *how
dare you* eyes, cradling her hand like I just took a hammer to it. I don't apologize, but lift the scroll out myself,
lightly, like a relic. The blackened edges flake under my
fingertips.

It doesn't feel like a mistake. It feels like a door
opening, and lungfuls of fresh air rushing in.

"What is it?" Cinzia asks.

I don't know what it is. I very much want to know,
but I do not want Cinzia to know, or Radan or George
or Ludmilla or anyone else milling around looking
mildly interested. "Nothing," I say, putting my violin

and bow away. I don't set the scroll down while I put on my coat and backpack, but switch it from hand to hand, having no doubt that Cinzia would snatch it and feel entitled to open it. In which case maybe I *would* take a hammer to her hand. I tuck the scroll into my inside jacket pocket, ignoring Cinzia's hooded glare.

"See you tomorrow," I say as a general announcement.

Radan is surprised. "Not coming to the party?"

"No," I say, because whatever is or isn't in the scroll, I am done with default Saturday nights, and Stooge's, and trying to block Cinzia from sitting on my lap, and spending the whole time imagining this alternate reality where a porcelain doll with voodoo eyes might be drinking tea in an oarless boat coursing down the Vltava with a parasol open to keep off the snow.

Or, you know, something slightly more likely than that.

6

Carpe Noctem

I consider the bathroom for privacy to look at the scroll, but the door's in view of the lounge and Cinzia is still watching me with narrowed eyes, so I leave the theater. It's snowing. I pause on the steps to glance at the flyer that caught Zuzana's eye earlier.

It's gone.

It was a red page with a phone-number fringe at

the bottom. Hanging in its place now is a sheet of white paper with one ragged margin. Torn from a notebook? It's unlined, so: a sketchbook. Something is written in tiny letters right in the center. I have to lean in close and squint to read it. It says:

Watch with glittering eyes
the whole world around you
because the greatest secrets are always
hidden in the most unlikely places.
Those who don't believe in magic
will never find it.

—Roald Dahl

And I know, I know it's for me. A message. But what am I meant to see? I look out over the street, taking in bent-headed figures hurrying through the snow. No one catches my eye. A slice of river is visible as blackness in a gap between two buildings, and the lights of the castle cast a glow on the underbelly of the crouching sky. The falling snow is light powder spun by gusts, like a dance out of *The Nutcracker*. If there's anything specific I'm supposed to see, I don't know what it is, but I know that my eyes are open, and I'm not sure they're glittering, but the world is.

I take the page down, careful not to rip it as I unstick the tape and roll it up to join the scroll in my jacket, then rush across the street to a pub, where I don't even order a drink or sit down at a table. I hope I won't be lingering. I grab the scroll out of my jacket and slip the black satin ribbon off, and . . . I unroll it.

And there she is.

A beautiful drawing of a beautiful face. Her big, dark eyes look wide and expectant. She's not smiling, but she's not *not* smiling, either. No voodoo blood-freeze. There's warmth there, and she's looking right at me. I mean, it's a drawing, of course (if she did it, and

I assume she did, then she's really talented), but it's a drawing *for me*, and it seems to shoot a spark at me like real eye contact. With eye contact, the intensity of spark is due to . . . I don't know, chemistry, whatever that really means. There are degrees of zing and tingle, depending on the eyes in question, and though these are just graphite renderings of eyes, there is zing. There is tingle.

At first the face is all I see, but then I realize what it is I'm looking at. What it is that she's given me. Her face is in the center, but the whole page is covered in a diagram: streets and landmarks, carefully drawn and labeled. My first thought, seeing the scroll tied with ribbon, had been that it looked like a treasure map, and . . . it is.

It's a treasure map. And the treasure? There she is, in the center of the page, the *X*-marks-the-spot.

Zuzana is the treasure.

I have a dark thought that it's a joke, that one of my friends has done this, but I dismiss it. None of my friends can draw. Besides, none of them even know I want to know her. I haven't mentioned her, for fear of pubescent-caliber backstage hijinx, and I don't *think* I stare at her. (When anyone's looking.)

No. It's got to be real.

So I do that awkward thing you do when you get good news in the company of strangers and you look around at them, grinning like an idiot, and they look back, *not* grinning like idiots, and you almost have to tell them, to tell *someone*. You almost hold up your piece of paper and say, "The girl I like just gave me a treasure map to herself."

But you don't. You just don't.

So I don't.

(Okay, so I *do*, but I immediately want to take it back. The knot of strangers is unmoved by my joy. In fact, I think that guy with the hat is the Enemy of All Happiness and might follow me and try to kill me.)

Pull yourself together, Mik. You have a map to follow.

I turn my back on the Enemy of All Happiness (on

the principle that most people who look like they want to kill you probably won't) and study the map. My map. Because it's for me. From Zuzana. Nope, not gloating. Just stating the facts in case you tuned out for a minute and missed it. Zuzana made me a map to herself.

And in a little speech balloon emanating from between her lips is written, in tiny letters:

Carpe noctem.

Seize the night.

And I blink and feel a surge of certainty and excitement, because of course that's what one does when one wants something. One seizes it.

Well, maybe not all things. Cats, for example, do not respond well to seizure. Probably girls don't, either. So this might not be a good credo in life, but for Saturday nights in general and this one in particular, it works.

My eyes keep returning to Zuzana's face. There's a smile pending, I think: the faintest tug at the left corner of her mouth, captured like a smile on pause. I want to unpause it and watch it unfurl. So how do I do that?

Where do I go? Words. Places. Focus, Mik. Stop grinning.

Find her.

I'm in Malá Strana now. The marionette theater is in Little Quarter Square, in the shadow of the Church of St. Nicholas, and the map is of Old Town, so I head across the river.

The Charles Bridge is one of those places that never gets old. Day or night, sun or snow, it's always different, the view on both banks of the Vltava like something out of a medieval engraving. On second thought, it actually does get old when it's crammed with tourists, which is pretty much all sunlit hours for most of the year, but it's quiet now, just a few scattered folk hurrying both ways between the rows of statues, like running a gauntlet of saints. I have this notion that any minute the saints could reach out their great stone arms to swat passing butts, and I realize that I'm giddy.

And nervous.

The map indicates a site in the mazelike heart of Old Town, which I know well but not well enough to remember what this particular place might be. I walk, and the closer I get, the more my nerves tighten like violin strings. Will it be a cafe, maybe, or a pub? Will she be waiting at a table? Somehow I can't picture her just sitting there. It's too mundane. The treasure map, the quote, the night of soft snow . . . it all portends something odder than that. So I'm not really surprised when I get there—pausing before rounding the corner to draw a deep breath—and find . . . no Zuzana.

The site is not a cafe or a pub. It's a tourist trinket shop of the sort that is ubiquitous in this quarter, all of them full of the same Mucha prints and cheap marionettes and gaudy Bohemian crystal. It's closed and dark, as one would expect at this time of evening, and I turn in a circle, looking around.

Watch with glittering eyes the whole world around you. . . .

I watch. I see a black cat slip through an open door across the street and have a brief impulse to follow it, as if it might be a feline escort doing Zuzana's bidding. I smile, glad no one can read my thoughts. Zuzana probably can't command cats with her mind. Probably.

I keep looking.

There are a couple of posters taped to a door, but they're for an absinthe tasting already past and a tour of Bohemian castles yet to come. Graffiti on the sidewalk, but it's just soccer propaganda. Nothing else catches my "glittering eyes."

I examine the map, but I'm pretty sure I've read it right.

Is this a joke? Could she be messing with me?

Of course she's messing with me. The real question is: Is she messing with me for good or evil, and am I a fool for playing along? I could just shrug right now and go meet my friends at Stooge's.

The thought makes me laugh out loud. As if.

I have an instinct about Zuzana. I think she's not good or evil, but both—the perfect mixture of the two, a swirled ice-cream cone of good and evil—and she wouldn't have led me here for no reason. There's something I'm not seeing.

But what? I'm just standing here with my hands in

my pockets, wondering what I'm missing, when I hear a tap. It's faint, at the glass shop window behind me—the place on the map—and the hair lifts on the back of my neck as I turn toward it.

The greatest secrets are always hidden in the most unlikely places.

And what unfolds after that . . . well, it makes cat-mind-control seem feasible.

7

Carpe Diabolus

There are marionettes, and there are marionettes. The Czech Republic has a long history of puppetry as art; it's a part of our national character, and puppets are part of the set-dressing of Prague. They're everywhere: hanging in shop windows, museums, theaters, street stalls. And most of what you see? By far most of what you see—particularly in shops like this—are not artisanal puppets from masters' workshops, like the ones at the theater. These are tchotchkes, tourist junk, mass-produced, forgettable. Clowns and princesses and knights, their heads round balls with features painted on. And that's what these are like.

Except for one.

I didn't see it before because . . . I wasn't really looking. A failure of "glittering eyes," I'm ashamed to say. The first thing is, it's not inside the window. It's outside, in front of the glass, behind which hangs a rack of humdrum tchotchke puppets. I guess I just took it for part of the store's display. Of course they wouldn't leave a puppet like this outside to be snowed on or stolen; I see that now. Because this puppet isn't humdrum. It's a beauty, of a quality one just does not find in a shop like this.

Oh. And also? It's kicking at the window with its heel.

So there's that.

Tap tap.

At first, it gives me a start for the reason one might expect: Because if a puppet is moving, then someone is moving it, and I assume that person must be Zuzana, and so I assume that she is here. I flush and feel my pulse stutter, and I try to gather my stammering wits in expectation of finally meeting her. But that's just the first instant. Because in the second instant, I find the fault in this assumption.

No one is moving this marionette. No one could be. Its crossbar is hooked to the upper window frame in full view, and its strings are slack. Even as its foot taps, its strings are slack, so that it appears to be moving its leg under its own power. Which is absurd, of course, so my mind smoothly transitions to a new assumption: that this puppet is mechanical. Remote-controlled, or something. Which is weird, but, you know, less weird than the alternative.

Well, whatever its method of movement, now that it's gotten my attention, its leg falls still. I take a step closer, examining it. Examining *him*. I find myself thinking of the puppet as a "him." He's one of the most iconic of Czech characters: none other than the devil himself.

He's got a polished mahogany look: smooth, dark wood, cunningly carved and splendid, with a goat's horns and beard, and goat legs tufted with cottony black fur. He's a St. Nicholas Day *cert* (devil), to be specific, identifiable by his sack. You see, in the Czech Republic, on December fifth, St. Nicholas goes around bringing candy and small gifts to children, accompanied by an angel and a devil. In a holiday tradition that is the stuff of nightmares, the devil threatens to scoop bad children into his sack and carry them to hell. (And you thought coal in your stocking was harsh?)

It's not uncommon for actors playing the *cert* to actually scoop small children into their sacks.

Uh-huh. It happened to me. I couldn't have been older than four. It may even be my earliest memory. The sack was scratchy and smelled like earth; inside, the darkness was total. I screamed myself hoarse; it probably lasted less than a minute, but I remember the terror as sprawling, unending. The *cert* was my uncle in coal-face, and my mother was not pleased with him. By way of apology, he gave me my first violin. It was only a toy, but it became my immediate favorite thing in life, and I sawed at it and sawed at it until my father couldn't take it anymore and bought me a real one, and lessons.

I have been known to say that the devil gave me my first violin. It's not even a lie.

So far, the *tap tap* is the only hint that this puppet might be my reason for being here, but on closer examination, I see that he has a small note peeking from his jacket pocket like a handkerchief. And on it, more of the tiny writing that is becoming familiar.

Carpe diabolus.

First, *seize the night.* Now, *seize the devil.* It *is* for me, then, if the creepy tapping had left any real doubt. For a moment, standing there, I feel the full experience of this night wrap around me. The detail of it, the planning. It's like something out of a fairy tale, and the city looks strange and new and full of secrets, shadows as sharp as if they're laid down in paint, and light . . . light like halos and phosphorescence, fireflies and animals' eyes.

I reach up and "seize the devil," lifting its crossbar off the window frame, and I wonder: What now? I run my eyes over it, turn it around, looking for more writing. Nothing. I even take out the little handkerchief note, but there are no other words on it. There seems to be something in its sack, though, so I ease open the drawstring and look in. I half expect there to be a tiny child curled inside being abducted to hell, but there's only paper. Of course, when I draw the paper out, it is not "only" paper. Nothing about this night is "only" or "just." Everything is gilded and strange and ethereal, and so this is an origami butterfly, folded of floral Japanese paper embossed with gold. I turn it over, looking for writing on it and finding none, and have just concluded that I have to unfold it when . . .

. . . it takes flight.

It takes flight.

The origami butterfly lifts into the air, and I could almost tell myself the wind has blown it, except that

I'm holding it between my fingers and feel a tug of . . .
will . . . as it disengages. Its wings beat once, sending it
into a graceful upward spiral so that I tip my head back
to watch it hover there for an instant, looking astonishingly alive . . . and then it's apparently released by
whatever power lifted it, and it floats back down to me.

I'm almost afraid to catch it—*how, how did it do
that? How did* she *do that?*—but I do catch it. It's a
trick, I tell myself, marveling. It's "magic"—the kind
in quotes. Of course. Because that's the only kind of
magic there is.

There's a string tied to it or something.

Some kind of completely invisible string that puppeteers know about, and which has now vanished, leaving no trace. Vanishing puppet string. Is that a thing? I
don't think that's a thing. I turn the butterfly over and
over in my fingers, searching for an explanation, but
there's none to be had. Well. Except one.

Magic.

The kind *not* in quotes.

A little war commences in my brain, "rational self"
versus "hopeful self," cage match. I'm not religious; I
don't believe in things—not out of any determination

not to. It's more like a default setting: My brain is an inhospitable environment for belief, but I've always said—and really meant—that life would be more interesting if those unseen things were real (and dragons, too, please), and of course death would be less of a bummer if there were a heaven (hell not so much). I've just never been able to believe any of it. Right now, though, to some small but detectable degree, it feels like the pH balance in my mind is shifting. Like my skepticism is being neutralized. Hopeful self is sitting on rational self's chest.

I unbutton the devil puppet's coat. If there's a radio control mechanism or something inside him, the natural balance of my mind will be restored. If not, who knows?

Under the coat I find a wire armature. No, not an armature. It's . . . a birdcage. The puppet's body is a small birdcage, and where his heart would be there is a tiny yellow canary on a bird swing, rocking gently to and fro. I wouldn't be surprised if it chirped, or flew. It doesn't, though, and I feel through the rest of the puppet's clothes for some hidden mechanism that might account for that *tap tap* of his leg at the glass, but

devil-head bone connected to the neck bone

there's nothing. He's wood and wire, just a puppet, and that tapping leg just hangs from the bottom of the birdcage, no internal control device at all. Only the puppet strings could have moved it.

And the strings were slack.

Curious. (You know, if *curious* means "impossible" or "freaky" or . . . "*indelibly awesome*.")

And now my head feels all full of moonlight or starlight or something. Or snow. My head feels like a snow globe that's been shaken, and glitter is swirling around in it like unmoored stars.

I unfold the butterfly. On the white underside of the origami paper I find a rhyme and a small schematic.

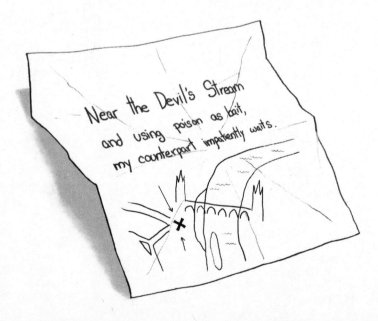

Okay. I'm good at riddles. The Devil's Stream is the canal where the Vltava flows around the Kampa, the island on the Malá Strana side of the river. As for "my counterpart," it could mean Zuzana's counterpart, but I don't know who that would be. If it's the devil's counterpart, though, it would be an angel, so I search my mind for some famous angel in that area but come up empty. As for "using poison as bait," I come up really, *really* empty.

So maybe I'm not good at riddles after all. Fortunately, there's the schematic, which shows a street, a tiny red *X* inscribed on it. A new destination, right back the way I just came.

Cradling the devil in the crook of my arm like a baby, I set off.

Whistling.

HER

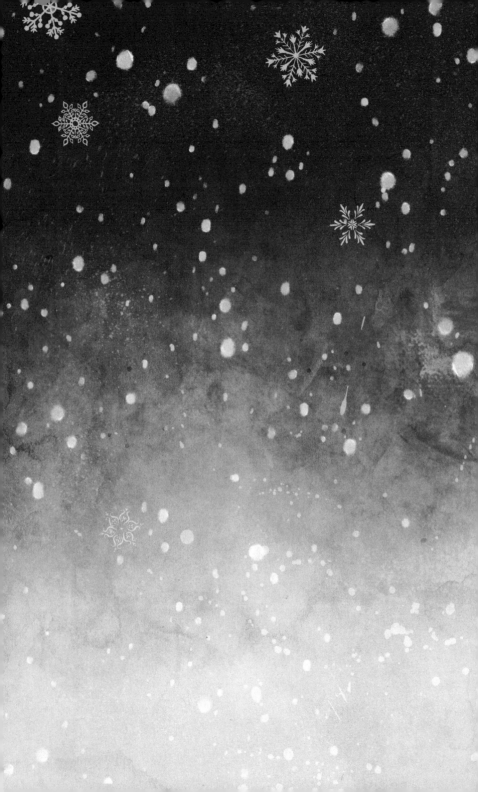

8

Thank God for
Murdered Monks

He came.

He came to find me.

When Mik rounds the corner out of sight, I sag against the wall of my hiding place—behind a lace curtain in the foyer of the building across the street—feeling as spent as if I've actually been conjuring spells and not just holding colored beads between my fingers. I let out a long breath.

Mik came to find me.

Did I think he wouldn't? I don't know. I don't know. I get too flustered around him to attempt anything like sustained eye contact, and without that, it's kind of hard to gauge interest. But watching him from hiding like a creepy serial killer, I could actually focus on his face long enough to believe that . . . he looked interested. Didn't he? Well, he always looks interested, he's that kind of alien, but just now he looked . . . dazzled.

"Don't you think he looked dazzled?" I ask the black cat that's rubbing against my legs. It slipped in here right when Mik showed up, like it was bloody well trying to lead him to me, and when it started purring as loud as a farm truck, I thought for sure Mik would hear. I may have shushed it. Shushed a cat. And what do you think it did? It purred louder.

"I will do just as you wish," said *no cat ever*.

In the safety of aftermath, though, my concern seems a little foolish. What did I think, that Mik would thrust open the door and demand, *"Why purrest thou, feline?"*

The cat continues its purr-fest, which I take to mean: Yes, Mik was definitely dazzled. How could he *not* be? I ensorcelled him. For which, thank you, scuppies. Two down. One for the tapping, one to lift the butterfly into the air. *Poof! Poof!* They go fast. I wish I had Karou's whole necklace. Karou. I text her: **Phase One a success. The Puppet That Bites would be proud.**

Because, yeah, using scuppies to animate a puppet, where on earth did I come up with *that* idea?

It's not copying, though. It's an homage. Of course, that's what artists always say when they steal from other artists. In this case, though, it really *is* an homage, to my own magical awakening two years ago. It seems right that Mik should be awakened in the same way. That we should lose our magic virginity the same way. To creepy puppets, during snowstorms.

(Okay. That sounds so wrong. But you know what I mean.)

The butterfly was my idea, though, and I think it was really the cherry on the cake, the thing that said, *Oh, you think this is a trick? So how am I doing* this, *smart guy?* I try to imagine what I'd think if it happened to me, but I can't. Once you know magic is real, it's really hard to remember what it was like not to know. It's kind of like trying to see how you look with your eyes closed.

(I did that once. I was a kid. It occurred to me out of nowhere to wonder what I looked like with my eyes closed, so I . . . um, went to the mirror and . . . closed my eyes.)

(Yeah. I looked exactly like the inside of a pair of eyelids.)

(I've never claimed to be a genius.)

I wait, giving the black cat a good scratch and letting Mik put some distance between us before I emerge from hiding. It's cold. I'm exhilarated. My heartbeat feels like a jaunty tune and my lips might as well be a parade float, and the rest of me just the little people on the ground holding the tethers.

Also, I'm starving, and I crazy have to pee.

I kind of wish I was just meeting Mik at Poison Kitchen. I mean, I *could*. I could just walk in behind him and say, "Well played, handsome man. Now let us eat strudel and then kiss. Just as soon as I get back from the bathroom."

But I'm not done dazzling him yet. I have more

scuppies to spend before we reach the talking portion of the evening. I'm hoping the talking portion is just a thin layer between the dazzling portion and the kissing portion, like the frosting between layers of a cake.

(Mmm. Cake.)

Not that I'm not keen to talk to him. I *am*—in the fantasy version of tonight, anyway, in which I actually manage to string words into sentences, and not just random magnetic-poetry sentences, but sentences that don't lead to the logical conclusion that I have brain damage. It's just . . . I can't begin to account for the intensity of my urgency to get kissing. The most likely explanation, after long thought, is that I'm a clone preprogrammed to perform this activity *now* or self-destruct.

Or else it's just Mik's velvety sweetness. Like a cupcake, in boy form.

I start walking, pausing to peer around the corner and make sure he's gone. I proceed toward the Malá Strana, stopping in a cafe on the way to alleviate the more pressing of my physical urges (neither lips nor stomach, no; nothing trumps the bladder), and then continue on, hurrying, but careful to scan the way ahead and make sure I don't overtake my stalkee. I don't see any sign of him, though, and amuse myself by wondering which set of footprints through the snow on the Charles Bridge might be his.

Those? Maybe.

When I feel a surge of fondness for Mik's maybe-footprints, I know I'm in serious trouble. The fact that I can't even muster any true self-disgust tells me how deep this goes. I'm doomed.

It's about the time I'm creeping into the courtyard of Poison Kitchen—under the archway draped in black frozen ivy, into the garden of medieval tombstones where the murdered monks lie buried—that I start to wonder if I'm being creepy. I mean, I am creeping. Does creep-*ing* automatically make one creep-*y*? Or are there dispensations for . . . romance?

I bet all stalkers believe they're being romantic. *I did it for love, officer.*

Have I crossed the line? I'm about to peer in through a window at Mik. For some reason, this feels worse than peering *out* a window, as I was just doing with a fairly clear conscience. After all, Peeping Toms peep *in*, not *out*. But this is still a public space, I argue to myself. I'm not peeping in *his* window. I would never do that. This is a cafe. Moreover, it's kind of *my* cafe. Mine and Karou's. In no legally recognized way, of course. We don't own it, except spiritually.

Which is a much higher court than actual real estate ownership. So I creep, totally uncreepily, up to the window.

And . . . there are . . . there are some little downy black feathers on the ledge. I know whose they are. Whose they *were*. Kishmish used to come here and tap at the glass to summon Karou. I get a lump in my throat remembering his little charred body falling still in Karou's hands, and these feathers serve as a reminder of how simple my life is, how lightweight this evening is, and how un-life-threatening the consequences of failure. It also reminds me of my duty to provide Karou with a rabid fairy tale, so I look through the window boldly, ready to make some magic.

And just as I see Mik, right where he's supposed to be, someone says my name. Well, not my name. A version of my name. "Zuzachka?" From behind me, in the courtyard.

Only one person calls me that, if he even deserves the designation "person," which he doesn't. Only one *jackass* calls me that, and I feel the cool of venom spreading through me, ready for deployment. Patience. I don't turn to respond yet, because I'm watching Mik, who is right this very moment sitting on a velvet settee at Pestilence—Karou's and my spiritual domain, which had been kept waiting for him by way of a RESERVED sign and a lovingly carved angel puppet—and *I need to make magic happen right now.*

"What are you doing?" asks jackass-voice.

My hand is already in my pocket. My fingers find a scuppy. Mik's facing the new puppet like it's a friend who saved a seat for him. It's the counterpart to the devil (which he's holding in his lap): an angel of the same proportions. I made them last semester, for a St. Nicholas Day performance for my Puppetry grade, which of course was an A.

I make the wish. I can't see it come true, but the bead vanishes between my fingertips and I know from the way Mik rocks back in surprise that something has happened.

Whereas the devil has a little canary on a swing

where its heart would be, the angel has a heart-shaped hole carved in its chest, and in it, a sparkler . . . which has just ignited, turning its heart into a mini-firework. In the show, I had to light it with a match. In this case, I wished it alight. I hope it looks fancy. I can't really see it from here, though, and anyway, with that done, I have less pleasant business to attend to. I turn around.

"What do *you* want." No question inflection. Nothing but sticky, poisonous disdain.

For Kaz. Kazimir Andrasko, Karou's disaster of a first boyfriend. First and last. Her despoiler. She thinks I don't know, but I know. And let me tell you something about me. I love vengeance like normal people love sunsets and long walks on the beach. I eat vengeance with a spoon like it's honey. In fact, I may not even be a real person, but just a vow of vengeance made flesh. My parents swear I was a real baby and not a demonic bargain, but of course they would say that. Bottom line: There is enough spare vengeance in me to act on behalf of mistreated, undervalued, toyed-with girls everywhere, and this is *Karou* we're talking about.

On behalf of Karou, Kaz has achieved the rarefied status of Nemesis First Class, but has not yet been

← sparkler that can be replaced in a chunk of wax

Cloth/pad legs

wooden feet

subjected to his personalized, Zuzana-tailored Scheme of Total Annihilation.

Yet.

"Just saying hi," he says, looking taken aback, like he actually thought I'd be happy to see him. "What's your *problem*?" he asks.

"What's my problem? I have so many, but violent tendencies and probable demonic origins are the ones that should concern you."

"Huh?" He gives me dumb-face, which is such a disappointing response to a good nemesis zinger. Kaz might deserve First Class status for Crimes of High Douchebaggery, but he's just not quality enemy material.

I sigh, and tell him so. "You are not a worthy opponent."

"What are you talking about? Opponent at what?"

"Opponent at *opponenting*. Duh. What are you doing here, Jackass?"

"What do you think? Is Karou here? Are you meeting her?"

I laugh. "You're not seriously looking for Karou," I say, but I see by the persistence of dumb-face that he is.

"She put you through a window the last time she saw you. Does that somehow leave room for hope?"

"She didn't know it was me when she did that," he argues. "What was up with her that night, anyway? Is she okay?"

Is Karou okay? No. No, she's really not, but in the scheme of her problems now, Kaz has become about as significant as a gnat inhaled by god. *Snuff.* I just shake my head. "Oh, Jackass," I say with what I hope comes across as gentle pity. "Poor Jackass. Let me explain something. You know in fairy tales, when a bunch of princes all try to win the princess's hand, but they're all vain and entitled and self-involved and they fail at the task and get put to death? And then there's one who comes along who's clever and good and he wins and gets to live happily ever after with her? Yeah, well, you're the first kind." I pat him on the shoulder. "It's all over for you."

Still dumb-face. And then he says, "You mean she's seeing someone else?"

"Oh my god!" I can only laugh. "Talking to you is like playing catch with a toddler. Get out of here, Kaz. Did you think I was kidding before? You're not welcome here. Imrich *will* put you in a coffin, and I *will* nail it shut."

The tables in Poison Kitchen are actual coffins, and the one-eyed owner, Imrich, is fond of me and Karou. We've been coming here at least three times a week for two and a half years. We painted murals in the bathrooms in exchange for goulash. Imrich is on our side.

"Right," says Kaz, rolling his eyes, not believing— or fearing—it for a second. "Let's go in, then. I hope you have your coffin nails ready." And he takes a step toward the door, calling my bluff.

Damn. It.

It's not a bluff! Imrich will do it. He's not entirely sane. I mean, look at his cafe! It's full of gas masks and skulls, for god's sake. Real ones. He will totally put Kaz in a coffin, and yes, he does have coffin nails. Like everything else in Poison Kitchen, they're antique, and authentic. He says they're from the coffins exhumed in Kutná Hora after some monk sprinkled Golgotha dirt there in the Middle Ages, making it the most popular graveyard in Central Europe. Most popular graveyard, what a thing! You'd only get to stay in the ground for so long before they'd dig you up to make room for the

POISON

KITCHEN

next guy. And—oh! Then in the late nineteenth century they hired some wood carver to make art out of all the dug-up bones. It's *awesome*. Imagine afterlife as part of a skeleton chandelier. *For real.*

The point is: coffin nails, *check*. Coffin, *check*. Crazy one-eyed Imrich and his bar cronies ready to take hold of pretty boy here and introduce him to the satiny interior of a hexagonal box?

Check.

Me, able to participate? *Not* check.

Any other night. Any. Other. Night. But tonight is not for vengeance. I take a deep breath. It's for a dazzling.

I do not look to the window. I so strenuously don't look to the window that my neck feels turned to concrete. I'm dying to know what's going on with Mik, but I don't want Kaz to catch me looking. He could mess everything up. I'm on a carefully calibrated schedule here.

Has Imrich brought Mik's tea yet? That's the plan. Pestilence—Karou's and my table, tucked under the giant equestrian Marcus Aurelius statue—was to be kept clear by a RESERVED sign, the angel puppet sitting there with its legs crossed on the velvet settee, and when—*if*—Imrich saw a guy come in and sit there, he was supposed to bring him a tea tray. Mik's last clue will be tucked in the arsenic bowl. (The *sugar* bowl, that is. Tea at Poison is served in antique silver services, the cream and sugar dishes engraved *arsenic* and *strychnine, hemlock, cyanide.* Cute, right?)

So basically, if Imrich has brought the tray, and Mik has found the clue, he could come through this door at any moment and I'll just be standing here, and Kazimir Andrasko will witness our very first words.

Nope. I've got to wrap up this snark-fight. "Actually," I tell Kaz, "I have other plans. But by all means, you go right ahead. And when you're trapped in there, in the dark coffin, hungry, thirsty, hallucinating, and desperate to pee, when the cafe's closed and there's no one left to hear your screams, just know . . . that I'm not thinking of you at all." I gesture to the door, and as the coup de grâce, I give him . . . Excited Maniac eyes. These are the eyes that say, *I have something fascinating to show you in the cellar. Come with me.* It's one of my favorite looks, and, incidentally, my brother's *least* favorite, because it's the one that invariably signals an escalation of hostilities to a level of dedicated vengeance that he could never match. He simply doesn't have it in him. Tomas knows:

You cannot defeat the Excited Maniac. You can only provoke her.

Kaz might not know this experientially, but he intuits it. The eyes freak him out. I see it. He quails. Glances at the door. Gives me that curled-lip look that bullies get when they're afraid of someone and trying to cover it up. He's going to call me a freak next. Wait for it.

"You're a *freak*, Zuzana."

"Yeah," I confirm with relish, amping up the eyes. *"I know."*

And that's it. He makes the decision. He turns and leaves. It's disappointing and satisfying at the same time. Disappointing because Kaz just came this close to getting coffined and I talked him out of it, and satisfying because I scared the big tool, and that's pretty much my mission statement.

With Kaz finally gone, I swivel toward the window—

—and see Mik headed my way! He's got the angel cradled in one arm, the devil in the other, and I have approximately three seconds to vanish into thin air before he opens that door.

That, or dive behind a tombstone.

Thank god for murdered monks.

9

Heart Hole

The door swings open, loosing the cafe din of voices and music into the courtyard, and then it shuts again, sucking back the noise like a cuckoo into a clock. Footsteps crunch across the snow. I can't see, and I'm fairly sure I can't be seen. I'm crouched behind a tombstone, just beyond the splash of light from the window, and as the sound of footsteps fades, I think two things:

1. Hiding behind tombstones *definitely* constitutes stalker behavior. and
2. Mik is en route to Location Three, and Location Three is *the final location*, the place where I am supposed to manifest my actual self and commence human interaction.

Do I have to? a voice in me whimpers. Can't the puppets act on my behalf? Puppet ambassadors? Yeah, because what's creepier than a stalker? A stalker ventriloquist who speaks through angel and devil puppets. I imagine Mik introducing me to his family: "I'd like you to meet my girlfriend Zuzana and . . . her representatives."

No no no. You can do this.

I can do this. I unfurl myself from behind the tombstone. I am the same person who just put fear in the heart of that best-friend despoiler, Kaz. *Rabid fairy, rabid fairy.* Why should speaking to a boy I like be so much harder than speaking to one I despise? I know it's all brain chemicals—*everything* is brain chemicals—but my excitement and dread feel like tiny wrestlers in my heart right now. I picture Excitement choking out Dread and gently, almost lovingly, lowering his inert body to the ground.

Go. Now. Leave Dread lying there. Go fast, before he gets up and sees which way you went. Breathe. Walk. Breathe. Walk. Look, Mik's footsteps. Follow them.

Breathe.

Walk.

Okay. I'm good. I'm going. I set my feet in Mik's footprints and feel a connection to him, like a total lunatic. Location Three isn't far, and it's a route I've walked hundreds of times, usually with Karou. Breathe. Walk. Mik's probably there already.

Do I know what I'm going to say to him?

Oh hell.

Dread rallies, chases us up the block. High-kicks Excitement in the neck just before I round the corner to Location Three. It stops me in my tracks, and I find myself stuck to the side of the building by the centrifugal force of my anxiety.

What am I going to say?

I fumble out my phone and text Karou: URGENT ASSISTANCE REQUIRED. WORDS. FIRST LINE. JUST SOMETHING SIMPLE THAT WILL MAKE HIM FALL INSTANTLY IN LOVE WITH ME. GO.

And then I wait, phone in my hand. And wait. The snow's coming down faster now, and my breath is a dragon's plume. The cold stone of the building seeps through my coat to turn my back to ice, and no message comes back from Africa.

Fine. I shove my phone back into my pocket. I know what I have to do. The Greek philosopher Epictetus said, "First say to yourself what you would be; and then do what you have to do." Good old Epictetus. I would be Confident Girl, and that means unplastering myself from the side of this building, for starters. It's my personal theory that only 27 percent of perceived confidence is actual confidence, and the rest is sham. The key is: If you can't tell the difference, there *is* no difference. Oh, the person shamming can feel the difference, in their clammy palms and pounding heart, but the outward effect—hopefully—is the same.

Words will come out of my mouth when the time

comes and I'll just have to hear what they are at the same time Mik does. There's no way to script this. (Or is there? Maybe I *could* write a script, and be in total control of our first conversation—No. No you cannot. Walk.) I set my body in motion. I feel Excitement and Dread hanging on to my ankles, but after a few steps I stop noticing, because I pass the point of no return. I round the corner into Maltese Square. There's the pink Baroque facade of the Lyceum. The courtyard gate, and beyond it only shadows. I can't see Mik, but . . . Mik can see me. I walk.

Location Three is the courtyard of my school. It's a pretty place, with a frozen fountain in the center and a marble bench carved to look like mermaids are holding it on their shoulders. The gate's left unlocked at night so students can use the studios as late as they need, but on a Saturday night this early in the term desperation levels are low, and there won't be anyone around. The courtyard's private but only semi-enclosed, which seems right. Intimate but not too intimate.

I stroll right up to the gate. That's not my heartbeat pounding in my throat. That's *confidence.*

The gate's standing open. I see Mik's footsteps.

I falter.

Because Mik's footsteps, they go in, and . . .

. . . they come back out.

They lead *away*.

And when I look into the courtyard, this is what I see: On the mermaid bench, my angel and my devil are locked in an embrace.

And Mik is not here.

I look around, over both shoulders, across Maltese Square. I stop just short of looking *up*, as if he might have flown away. He's nowhere.

He left.

Inside me: a desert of disappointment.

Mortification.

Paralysis.

Bewilderment.

And humiliation.

I hate humiliation. I want to kick humiliation in its measly toothpick shins.

I stand here for a minute before I realize that Mik could be watching from somewhere close by, and that

thought propels me into the courtyard. I don't step in his footprints now, but skirt them like I'm scorning them. *Jerk footprints, take that.* My heart feels *zested.* Finely shredded and ready to add to cake batter. It doesn't hurt, because it's not there anymore. Like the angel's chest, with her empty heart hole—but without the sparkler.

So very without the sparkler.

I stop in front of the puppets, and there's a blankness in my mind as I stare at them. He posed them like lovers. How mean. I would never have guessed that Mik was mean.

And then I see that the ice orb is gone. I'd hung it from the arbor that arches over the bench. The final artifact on this treasure hunt: a smooth chunk of clear ice about the size of a baseball, and frozen inside it, rolled up and tucked into a little plastic tube, is one last message. The idea was that by the time the ice melted, I'd be ready for Mik to read it, ready for the talking portion of the evening to transition to the next portion. You know which portion I mean. Oh god. My lips are bereft, like they've been left at the altar. They were so sure how this night was going to end.

Did Mik take the ice orb with him? Why would he do that? I look around to see if it might have fallen, but it's not here, and . . . I start to get mad. He shouldn't have taken it. If he was going to leave, he should have left the message, too. I don't want it at large in the world for him to read and laugh over and show to his friends.

(*He wouldn't do that*, a voice in me insists, like I know him at all.)

(You do *know him.)*

I don't. Of course I don't. We've never even spoken. But I was pretty confident that he wasn't a jerk. That he wasn't a *jackass*. Not that this is on par with what Kaz did to Karou, of course, but it's not great, either. I was fully prepared for him to not show up at Location One. I'd have been really disappointed, yeah, but I couldn't have held anything against him. If he's not interested, he's not interested. But why follow the treasure hunt to the end, looking all dazzled and velvety the whole time, and then . . . run away?

My phone buzzes. It's from Karou: a list of conversation openers that I won't be needing.

—a) Hi. I'm Zuzana. I'm actually a marionette brought

to life by the Blue Fairy, and the only way I can gain a soul is if a human falls in love with me. Help a puppet out?

—b) Hi. I'm Zuzana. The touch of my lips imparts immortality. Just sayin'.

—c) Hi. I'm Zuzana. I think I might like you.

I read them with bitterness, then drop down onto the bench and nudge the puppets apart, breaking their embrace. The angel falls back, her arms askew, head lolling off the edge of the bench in a swoon. Dead of a broken heart. *I think I might like you* indeed. No dancing around it, just honesty. That's what Confident Girl would say. If she had someone to freaking say it to.

I write back: Thanks, but I won't be needing these after all.

—What? Why?

—. . . he ran away. . . .

—???

—Left the puppets. Left them MAKING OUT and didn't wait around for me. At least the puppets got some action tonight.

There's a pause during which I imagine Karou getting outraged. But when she writes back, it isn't outrage that comes through.

—This makes no sense, Zuze. Did he leave a note or anything?

A note? I didn't think of that. A spark flickers in my heart hole. Is it possible?

Heart hole.

Heart hole! The angel's heart hole. Something's poking out of the angel's heart hole! I look up, around, as if Mik might be spying on me the way I've been spying on him. But I don't think so; there's nowhere to hide. I reach out . . . it's a rolled-up paper. I unroll it and, in a second, all my disappointment, mortification, paralysis, bewilderment, and humiliation evaporate and are replaced by . . . giddiness, relief, thrill, swoon, and delight.

It's Mik's own version of my first treasure map, hastily done. At its center: a ballpoint-rendered self-portrait that is pretty much a child's smiley face doodle with sideburns and a goatee. As bad as it is—and it *is*—there's something so sweet about it, something so totally affectless and jerk-free that I can't believe I ever thought Mik would do something mean. *Oh ye of little faith.* I remember the conversation I had at Poison with Karou a while back, before I even knew Mik's name, where I wondered what chance there was of him being a non-orifice. As if there could be any doubt! He radiates non-orificeness. I was just afraid to believe it—or else afraid that some other girl was already the lucky beneficiary of his non-orificeness.

Which doesn't appear to be the case—because he played my game tonight, and now . . . he's inviting me to play *his*.

The puppets' embrace takes on new meaning, and my cheeks go hot. Was it a message? How could it not be? The scroll is a message, too: A speech bubble balloons from smiley-Mik's lips. It reads:

And there's a crudely drawn map of the Kampa, but no *X*-marks-the-spot that I can see. The Devil's Stream isn't very long, but it's certainly long enough that a precise location would be helpful. And what's with the twenty minutes? What's he up to?

Intriguing . . .

My phone is vying for my attention. It's a string of texts from Karou, all along the lines of: Hello? Z???

My fingers are shaking a little with thrill shivers as I type back: You're a genius and a savior. THERE IS A NOTE! <3 <3

I have never in my life typed a heart symbol. Those are for milquetoast girls. Karou will probably think my phone's been stolen—or possibly my body, by a lovelorn alien. I send the text anyway.

This is what comes back: . . . who is this??

Me: Don't you dare mock me.

Karou: You're not going to start collecting heart-shaped rocks or anything, are you? Because we might have to renegotiate our friendship.

And I have some time to kill before the mysterious twenty minutes elapse, so I call her—stupid texting, anyway; sometimes it takes a ridiculously long time to think of actually dialing the phone and speaking instead of typing away like numbskulls—and I assure her emphatically that there is no heart-shaped rock collection in my future. "Toes," I say, thinking of my grandfather's supposed golem souvenir. "I'm going to take toe trophies from all my boys from now on," and if Karou knows that "all my boys" so far equals *zero boys*, she doesn't let on.

"That's more like it," she says.

It's really good to hear her voice. She tells me she's going to Pakistan next. Pakistan! I issue all sorts of ill-informed warnings that she doesn't need, like to wear a burqa and not do any random sexy dancing in public, and she keeps trying to bring the conversation back to me and Mik.

Me & Mik.

I've never been part of an ampersand before. Never a "we," never an "us," but by the time I get off the phone and start walking—slowly, as directed—in the direction of the Devil's Stream, I'm feeling pretty good about my chances. It may be a grand delusion, but the feeling carries me along like I'm floating, and in no time at all, I'm nearing the footbridge at the end of Velkoprevorske Street, wondering where to go next. And that's when I hear it.

Music.

10

Peacock Footprints

Violin. Live and real and drifting with the snow. It's *Eine kleine Nachtmusik*, which I've heard so many times that I didn't even realize, until hearing it now, that it had become . . . mundane. *Oh, yeah, Mozart's such a genius. What's for dessert?* But hearing it like this, outside, at night, in a snowfall and meant for *me* . . . it's newly born in my mind as the sublime creation that it is. It's the Andante, softer and sweeter than the Allegro, and it's just . . . I can't even explain it.

It's a dimension. The space around me, the world above me—until just now a void of night air beset by snow flurries—becomes a living thing. Music. Close your eyes and it's a rosebush blooming in time lapse so that its shoots and blossoms flow outward in a swift choreography of growth and collapse, twine and coil, release and fade.

Close your eyes and music paints light vines and calligraphy on the darkness within you.

It draws me forward, like a hand extended. Mik is on the other side of it, somewhere as yet unrevealed, his music making a trail straight to him, and I'm so grateful in the moment that it's not an ordinary person I've fallen for, and not even an ordinary musician, but a violinist.

As soon as I step onto the footbridge I see him. There's the mill wheel just beside the bridge—the cute wooden mill wheel every tourist to Prague snaps a photo of—and Mik is down on the narrow dock beside it, barely ten feet away. There's a wall between us, though, concrete topped with an iron fence, and my miniature self has to stand on tiptoe to peer through the bars. His head, cozied by his knit cap, is bent over his violin, his posture is loose and fluid, he's blushing his blush of exertion and creation, and nothing has ever been quite as amazing as the fact that this perfect sound is the result of the smooth, deliberate swing of this beautiful boy's arm.

I'm not the only person who's been drawn to the music. Passersby are stopping to listen. Some windows clatter open in the buildings fronting the stream, and for a minute everyone is still, bent toward this lovely sight: Mik on the mill dock, playing Mozart to the snow.

No, not to the snow. To *me*.

Eine kleine Nachtmusik is Mozart's Serenade 13. Serenade.

World, I think it's important to acknowledge here that I am being serenaded. The Charles Bridge arcs in the backdrop, its lampposts ghostly. The canal is black and glinting, and the night is saying: *Yep. Everything is miraculous.*

Indeed, Picasso. Indeed.

"Excuse me," I say to a couple who are paused

nearby, leaning into each other so that their breath plumes mingle and become one. "Can you boost me up?" I gesture to the wall. It's high, with pointy iron finials to further discourage what I am about to do, but the couple make no effort to dissuade me. They smile like they're in on a secret, and the guy makes a stirrup with his hands, and up I go. That's when Mik looks up. Right when I'm balanced on top of the wall.

Our eyes meet, and all this rigamarole and scheming, the back-and-forth across the bridge and diving behind tombstones, it all comes down to this moment.

Our eyes meet.

And . . . it's like all my life I've been this tower standing at the edge of the ocean for some obscure purpose, and only now, almost eighteen years in, has someone thought to flip the switch that reveals that I'm not a tower at all. I'm *a lighthouse*. It's like waking up. I am incandescent. I never knew I could emit heat and light. *Damn*. If the music created an external dimension, this creates an internal one.

There is more to me than I knew.

Mik smiles, and it's such a mix of *glad* and *shy* and *sweet* and *eager* and even a little bit of what I could swear is *amazed*—like he's amazed by his good fortune that *I* am climbing over a wall to him—that it triggers a kindred smile in me. My face responds without authorization from my brain, so the resulting smile feels like the biggest, most unguarded, goofiest smile I've ever unleashed in my entire life. I didn't even know my face could *do* this. It's like there were hidden zippers in my cheeks. Jesus.

This must be what *feelings* are. This is why people write poems! I get it now.

I get it, and I want more.

I start to climb down the outside of the bridge. Or, well, I look down for clues as to how I might accomplish this last, crucial step to finally entering Mik's magnetic field, but it's a far drop to the little metal walkway below, and I hesitate. And no sooner do I hesitate than Mozart hesitates. By which I mean, Mik's bow falters over the strings and the music cuts off, and when I look back up, he's laying his violin and bow in their case and coming toward me. There's a light smattering of applause, but I'm not going to be distracted by anything outside the circle of this moment.

Here's the situation. Me: clinging to the outside of

the bridge. Mik: on the metal walkway below. His head is about even with my feet. He's looking up at me, and our eyes meet again and I'm thinking *I love your face* at him because it's just the best face and I can't help imagining a situation in which we are standing with our foreheads and nose tips touching, and it's only now that I realize the lighthouse radiance I feel myself emitting is actually *blushing*. He's blushing, too, and with the distance reduced between us there's the sensation that our blushes are meeting in the middle. The edges of our magnetic fields are bumping against each other.

And then Mik speaks. All he says is "Hi," but he says it like he's breathing it out on a plume of pure awe, and it melts me.

"Hi," I say back. A word spoken, and no mouth malfunction. Granted, it's only *hi*, but it's the most meaningful *hi* I've ever said, and it doesn't even sound like my voice. It sounds like it belongs to some girl with a heart-shaped rock collection, and I defiantly do not care. "Help me down?" I ask.

And he reaches for me. I crouch to sit on the edge of the concrete wall, the iron of the rail hard at my back. I find I'm still just a little out of range of Mik's hands, so I have to tip forward, fall to him and let him catch me. And I do. And he does. And it's like I'm watching myself do this thing—fall into Mik's waiting arms, into his magnetic field at last—from a great distance. He catches my waist, so padded by my sweater and coat that it's just pressure and not even the feeling of hands, and I catch his shoulders, likewise coat-padded but still nice and boy-shouldery, and he sets me down in front of him, simple and neat, and here we are, squarely arrived at the talking portion of the evening.

There's a long pause.

But it's not a bad pause, because Mik is looking at me like I'm the treasure from the high shelf that someone's just taken down and put into his hands. I find I don't mind being looked at like this. I don't mind it at all.

"I got your note," he says.

"I got yours, too."

"I can't draw," he says a little quickly, like he's offering an apology, and I know he's just as nervous as I am.

"And I can't play the violin," I counter. "That was . . .

beautiful." It's such an understatement. *Sublime* might begin to get at what it was, but that would just sound pretentious.

He shakes his head, humble. "That was nothing. I mean, don't tell Mozart I said that. But it wasn't like what you did tonight. I don't even know what to say. It's the coolest thing anyone's ever done for me."

"What, run you all over town in the snow?" It's my turn to act humble. It *was* really cool. I am well aware.

"Yeah, like that's all it was. I don't even know how you did some of that stuff." There's a brief pause before he adds, "But don't tell me. I want to just think it was magic."

"It *was* magic," I say simply. I've learned this from Karou, as regards magic: You can tell the most outlandish truths with virtually no risk of being believed.

Except, apparently, in the case of Mik. "I believe it," he says. "This is pretty much what I imagined your Saturday nights are like."

Pause. Consider. Unpause. "You imagined my Saturday nights?"

"Yeah," he says, with a gentle inflection of *of course*. "Every week when I'm doing something boring and typical after the show. It's how I punish myself for laming out and not talking to you—by imagining you doing, like, secret errands over the rooftops, or vanishing through trapdoors that leave no seam when they close, just traces of silver dust."

It's like he's describing Karou. Secret errands and vanishing and trapdoors? And it hits me that Mik thinks I'm mysterious.

It is, hands down, the best compliment I've ever been given. I could tell him what my Saturday nights are really like—that they're spent lolling at Poison Kitchen with Karou over sketchbooks and tea, moping about *him*—but I don't. I like this being-mysterious business. "Silver dust?" I inquire.

He shrugs, bashful. "I don't know. Or maybe peacock footprints."

This is interesting. "Peacock footprints," I repeat.

"This poem I read," he says. "It had this line about 'anyone who's woken up to find the wet footprints of a peacock across their kitchen floor,' and ever since, I've kind of wanted to. Um. Wake up and find peacock footprints."

"Okay," I say, going with it. Peacock footprints. *That*

could be arranged, I think, because I bet a scuppy could handle that, but then this sense of intimacy strikes me. It's the part about Mik waking up. The idea of . . . being there for that, and vice versa. It's like a glimpse of the future—a possible future, so far beyond my ken that I get a shiver up my spine. It's this feeling of being a kid in a roomful of grown-ups: All around you are just *knees*, and the grown-ups are up there in their own world, a bunch of distant heads talking about things you can't begin to understand.

Waking up with someone is the natural aftermath of *sleeping* with them, and that's something that happens up there, with the grown-up heads. Me, I'm still down here on the floor with the dropped Cheerios, getting thwacked in the face when the dog wags its tail.

Metaphorically speaking.

It's not a revelation, or any kind of decision to make. It's more a glimmer of decisions to come, soon or not soon. In adolescent fantasyland, the kiss is the happy ending. On the planet of grown-ups, I am fully aware, it's only a beginning.

I look at Mik intently, wondering where he falls in

the spectrum of adolescent versus grown-up expectations.

(And PS, if you use the word *grown-up*, you probably aren't one.)

"You're like that," he's saying. "Like peacock footprints. Unexpected. And this night was like that. Amazing. And . . . I didn't want to be the guy who just wakes up and finds the footprints."

"Wait. What? I thought you *did* want to find the footprints."

"I do, but not *just*. I wanted to do something, too. Contribute something. To this." He makes a gesture that encompasses us. An "us" gesture that, given the recent detour of my thoughts, seems rich with meaning. And then the gesture opens up to include the dock, the violin lying there, the stream going past. "Not that it's much. It was the best I could do on the spur of the moment."

"It's great," I say, meaning it completely. "It's totally peacock footprints. I didn't expect it at all." I don't mention the brief despair breakdown it caused back in the Lyceum courtyard, or my zested heart, or my argument with myself over whether or not he was a jerk.

"Good." With a little worry frown, he says, "I hope it didn't hijack your plans."

I shake my head. "No. This is great." What were my plans, anyway? I was going to play it by ear after the courtyard, with the thought of going somewhere indoors where the ice orb would begin to melt. Where *is* the ice orb, anyway? He hasn't already melted it, has he, and read the message? My heartbeat skitters at the thought. "Do you, um, have that . . . ice orb?"

"Oh. Yes. I do." He snaps upright, and I realize belatedly that he's been leaning down to bring his face nearer to mine. Now he offers me his arm like some kind of old-fashioned gentleman. "This way, please, my lady."

Hmm. What's this? I loop my arm through his, and he escorts me to the end of the dock, past his violin case, and reveals . . . more peacock footprints.

Not literally.

There's a rowboat tied up at the end of the dock, swaying gently below us in the dark water. In the most delightful and unexpected tableau, it's set up for tea. I recognize the tea tray at once as belonging to Poison. A silver teapot, "arsenic" dish and "strychnine" pitcher,

two white china cups on saucers, and there's the ice orb glinting like crystal, and also . . . a bakery box. Bakery box. Oh my god I'm starving. And freezing. And tea . . . and a bakery box . . . in a rowboat . . . I look up at Mik, in awe. "How did you—?"

"The twenty minutes," he says. "I walked really fast. But even so, I couldn't have done it if that crazy guy with the eye patch wasn't such a fan of you. I got the definite feeling that he wouldn't have let the silver out the door for anyone but you."

"Well, there is one other person. My best friend. We go there a lot. Imrich's kind of protective of us."

"You think? He gave me this ten-second silent stare, and I'm pretty sure that if my intentions weren't honorable, my face would have melted."

Hmm. I hope his intentions aren't *too* honorable. Wait. Or do I? I hope his intentions are mildly dishonorable, and extend to kissing, and that's all. For now. "I'm glad your face didn't melt." *Because you'll need it for kissing.*

"Me, too. Would you like some tea?"

"More than words can say."

There's a little ladder at the end of the pier and I climb down first and scramble into the boat, trying not to set it rocking and spill the tea. I'm light, anyway, so it doesn't move too much until Mik climbs down after me.

"So the tea's from Poison," I say, which makes sense. It *is* right around the corner. "What about the boat?"

"Well." Mik pours tea into my cup. It's still steaming, thank god. "Let's just say, we should probably keep it tied up where it is."

My first mouthful of tea is heaven, and the warmth of the cup in my numb hands is, too. "I see. So we don't have permission to be here."

"Not exactly. I only had twenty minutes. I was kind of scrambling. Cake?"

Cake. As subject changes go, it's a good one. I hesitate for the tiniest instant, though, because my brain gets on this hamster wheel of concern over the likelihood of imminent kissing. To eat or not to eat, that is the question: whether 'tis Nobler in the stomach to suffer the Slings and Arrows of outrageous Hunger (while keeping mouthparts in pristine kissing condition) or to take Spoon against a Slice of cake, and—

"Yes, please," my stomach pipes up. And Mik opens the bakery box to reveal a small, whole Sacher torte, its chocolate so dark it looks black. *Chocolate.* Thank god. If he'd brought a *non*-chocolate cake, I would have had to give him a demerit. We have no forks or plates, only our teaspoons, so we eat with those, me making the first divot in the cake's smooth surface—a dainty fairy-like bite that is really not my usual MO—and *holy hell* the chocolate is so intense and pure it should be named an element and given a spot on the periodic table. It would be *Ch*, which isn't even taken.

The boat sways softly, and my feet are freezing, but the tea warms me from the inside, and each little jolt of Mik eye contact triggers a minor blush that warms my face, so I'm doing okay (so much more than okay), even though it's February in Prague and only crazy people would sit in a rowboat eating cake in a snowstorm.

Because: oh. The snow's coming down thicker now. We both look up and around, like: *huh.* It's falling in great downy billows, and when it hits the water it melts like sugar in coffee. It would be very sweet coffee, because it's *a lot* of sugar. On the rooftops and dock—and even on the cake—it's piling up.

It's Mik who makes the decision to ignore it. "So, are you from Prague?" he asks me, looking at me with this determination to not notice the blizzard. He takes another bite of cake.

I take another bite, too. And another gulp of hot tea. "Český Krumlov. You?"

"Here. Vinohrady. My family still lives there, but I'm in Nové Město now."

We're both acting like we're at a table in a cafe, as normal as can be. "I live in Hradčany," I tell him, "with a vampiric great-aunt."

And this totally normal conversation unspools from there, covering the basics: family, siblings, school, favorite composers, favorite movies, favorite wood (for carving puppets), the prehistory of the sandwich, and whether the ancient Romans got their togas caught in the spokes of their unicycles.

Okay, so it *starts out* totally normal and takes a turn. On account of the ice orb.

Ah, yes, the ice orb.

See, while I'm not paying attention to it—because, hello, I'm paying attention to the beautiful boy who serenaded me and brought me cake—I guess it rolls up to rest against the hot teapot and . . . melts, and . . . yields up its message.

Ready or not.

HIM

11

Seize the Something

So, I'm really cold. The tea's helping a little, but it's getting silly, staying out here. At some point it'll go from silly in a good way to silly in a we're-going-to-be-found-like-this-in-the-morning-with-our-smiles-frozen-on-our-blue-faces way. The tea can be our hourglass. When we run out, or it gets cold, whichever happens first, it's time to go. But for the moment, the tea's still hot, and it's still good silly. A story we'll tell.

The night we finally met.

It's a really good story so far. I wonder how the rest of it will go. How it will end. The night, I mean, not the story. I know how I hope the night will end. Well. There are two versions, actually, but my better nature has locked my guy nature in a box on this one. My better nature hopes it will end with me walking Zuzana home and kissing her good night at her door.

I keep wanting to reach over and touch her face.

Hell. Seeing her shiver, I want to take her into my coat and button it around her. I want to warm my face against her neck and steam her up like a mirror and write my name on her with my fingertip. I want to warm my hands up, too. I think of her skin so deeply buried in there under coats and layers, and she's like the secret center of a Tootsie Pop. Something about winter layers: They challenge you to imagine the hidden shape within. I mean, it's not all imagination. I've seen Zuzana out of her outermost layers at least, at the theater, but I've only known her in winter, so: sweaters, scarves, jeans, boots. Nary a glimpse of ankle or clavicle, those miracles of girl geometry. It's very Victorian, but in the depths of a girlfriendless winter, a glimpse of ankle would probably excite me.

In the abstract, walking around the city with Zuzana's notes and maps in my pockets and her puppets in my arms, it was easy to not be such a guy. There was something so innocent about it, like a fairy tale. But sitting right in front of her, looking at her beautiful face, there are . . . impulses. If this night is a fairy tale, then this is the happily ever after, right, or at least the beginning of it? And the thing about happily ever afters? Those princesses and woodcutters' sons have bodies under their coats, too. I mean, what do you think happily ever after *means*?

(I can't be the only one who thinks this.)

And it's not like I've never imagined happily-ever-aftering with Zuzana. I'm a guy. But even before tonight, there was something about her that took my imagination to a higher level. A girlfriend level—like a movie montage of hand-holding and cooking dinners and reading books in the park.

And *then* happily-ever-aftering. Eventually. Someday. Maybe.

Hopefully.

Untying the sash of Zuzana's coat would be like taking the ribbon off a present.

Cut it out.

Okay. Better nature reasserted. I'm good. All this time we're talking, and it's easy. Zuzana's funny and quick—witty—and she rolls with random things like peacock footprints so that every thread gets woven in and every topic gets bigger, weirder, more fun. It's the best kind of conversation. We're laughing a lot. I tell her how I got kidnapped to hell when I was four. She tells me about the biting puppet. I want to meet this crazy grandfather of hers, and now I really want a golem toe, too.

And then I reach for the teapot to refill our cups one last time—the hourglass is up, the tea dregs are cold—and that's when I notice: The mysterious ball of ice Zuzana hung up in the Lyceum courtyard has melted into a puddle. Well, half melted. The side resting against the teapot has gone flat, and the capsule inside is sticking out.

"Oh." When I pick it up I see Zuzana go still, and I wonder: What's in it? When I look inquiringly at her, she's biting her lip. Nervous. "Should I open it?" I ask, and she doesn't answer right away.

Now I'm really curious. Her eyes consider me in silence—and more silence, and more—and I have this uncomfortable feeling that she's seeing right into my locked-away guy nature, and somehow knows I thought of her as a Tootsie Pop center, and then—silence, silence, silence—finally, cautiously, she says . . . "Okay."

"Okay?" I hold it up, the partial ice ball with this little tube sticking out of it.

"Okay," she repeats, and her eyes are very still and clear, very dark and watchful. This is something important.

I already can't feel my fingers, and freeing the tube the rest of the way from the ice deadens them to the point that they feel like wooden finger prosthetics, and if you've ever tried to open a plastic tube and unroll a very small scroll using wooden finger prosthetics (and really, who hasn't?), you know it's not easy. And the whole time I'm fumbling around with it, the silence between us gets thicker and deeper, like the snow.

At last, I manage it. I unroll the message, and read it.

Carpe puella.

Seize. Seize the something. Damn. I don't know what *puella* means. I know what I hope it means, but it's not like I speak Latin. *Noctem* and *diabolus* were easy, but now I'm the one biting my lip. "Um," I say.

And Zuzana is still watching me with the intensity of a mind reader. Her jaw is clenched. I am messing this up.

"I don't . . . I don't speak Latin?" I hear myself ask it like a question, and as soon as the words are out, as if by magic, the tension leaves Zuzana's face.

"Oh. Me, either. I had to Google that. I was afraid it might be too obscure. Here." She reaches for the scroll and I hand it over, and then she gets a pen out of her bag and hunches over the note, screening it from my sight as she writes something more on it. Then she rolls it back up and solemnly hands it over.

Now it reads:

Carpe puella Zuzana.

I swallow, and it's cartoonishly audible. "That was what I *hoped* it meant," I say. "But if *puella* meant, like, *sandwich*, or *bicycle*, it could have been pretty embarrassing."

There's a heavy pause from Zuzana, just long enough for me to realize how wrong of a response this is to a girl's request—or, rather, *command*—to seize her, and then she asks, calmly, "Are there even Latin words for *sandwich* and *bicycle*? I mean, did the Romans even have sandwiches and bicycles?"

"Well, sandwiches. There have always been sandwiches. The same aliens who brought dinosaurs to Earth brought sandwiches, too." *What am I saying?* Am I supposed to just lean across right now and reach for her? "I don't know about bicycles, though."

"I don't think they had bicycles," Zuzana says. "Just unicycles."

"Unicycles." I want to reach for her, but it seems so abrupt, I don't know, like there's a lunar logic to things like this, a pull of the moon, and the timing isn't right. "I did not know that. Did their togas get caught in the spokes?"

"All the time. There's even a mosaic of it in Pompeii."

"It happened to my sister," I say. "Not a unicycle, though. She was on the back of some guy's moped in Milan and her skirt got caught in the spokes, and it was this flimsy gypsy skirt and the whole thing just tore away from the waistband, so there she was, in just her underwear and waistband, on this chic, busy street in Milan while like a dozen bystanders tried to free her skirt from the moped tire."

"That's . . . mortifying."

"She also got hit in the head by a pigeon. Same day."

"A pigeon . . . pooped on her head?"

"No. No, it collided with her head. Actually knocked her off her feet and drew blood. She had to get shots, because of the risk of infection."

"Sounds like Italy was trying to get rid of her."

"Well, it worked. She left the next day and vows never to return."

So here we are, talking about Roman unicycles and alien sandwiches and my sister's Italian misfortunes, while hanging in between us is:

MY EPIC FAILURE TO CARPE.

What's wrong with me? Maybe I locked guy nature away too tightly. No, it's not that. Guy nature is not what's called for here. Zuzana deserves better than guy nature.

"Can I borrow your pen?" I ask her.

She hands it to me, and I bend over the little scrap of paper and write: *I want very much to carpe you*, it says. *I may try to surprise you, though, if that's okay. Also, I can't feel my face and hands.*

The writing is really messy, on account of not being able to feel my hands. I give the paper to Zuzana, and when she reads it, she laughs. "Maybe it's time to go."

It is definitely time to go. So we get out of the boat, wrangling the tea tray. I help Zuzana up the ladder first and then follow, and it's when I'm stooping on the dock for my violin case that I see . . . something completely crazy.

All evening, ever since *carpe diabolus*, my rational self has been lying on its back making lazy snow angels while hopeful self sits on its chest humming and I let myself play this game of magic. But it was still a game. I mean, I didn't really believe it, I guess, because all of a sudden . . . I do. This is no longer suspension of disbelief. It's *belief*, and the two things are water and wine.

In front of me, forming one by one on the smooth

pelt of the snow and leading fleetly away even as I watch, are footprints. For all my poetry quoting, I couldn't actually tell you what a peacock's tracks look like, but they probably look like this: like large-ish bird tracks. Like hieroglyphs.

Like magic.

I'm speechless. I turn to Zuzana, but she hasn't noticed. She's looking up at the sky, the snow swirling around her like feathers in a movie pillow fight, and I look back at the dock and already the tracks are vanishing beneath the new flurries—a secret sight no one will ever believe, maybe not even me tomorrow—and when I turn back to her, Zuzana is looking at me. Lacquer-dark eyes, choppy hair licked into spikes by the weather. Black coat, black boots, hands shoved in pockets. And that doll quality to her face that comes of being *fine*—fine as in museum-quality, every plane and curve like an artist's harmonious choice, this fullness offsetting that austerity, this angle enhancing that arch—and the heart shape, and the wide-set eyes, and the elegant dark brows with their extraordinary mobility, and the *smoothness*.

And the lips.

The lips. Who can ever say how these things happen? I think the moon is in charge of more than just tides. Either I've moved or Zuzana has moved, I'm not sure which. I only know that she's much closer all of a sudden, and whatever was hindering me from seizing her before has let me go. The space between us has vanished and I'm looking from her lips to her eyes and back again and she's doing the same with mine, and there's this instant as I'm leaning toward her that we both look from lips to eyes at the same moment and lock and it's so far beyond zing and tingle, this eye contact. It's like losing gravity and falling into space—the moment of pitching headlong when the endlessness of space asserts itself and there is no more down, only an eternity of up, and you realize you can fall forever and never run out of stars.

Her face, my hands. Zuzana's face is in my hands. My numb fingertips trace down her jawline and back into her hair—just far enough to curve around the column of her neck and—lightly, gently . . .

. . . seize her.

And kiss her.

. . .

. . .

. . .

And there's no better way to thaw a face, as it turns out, than with another face.

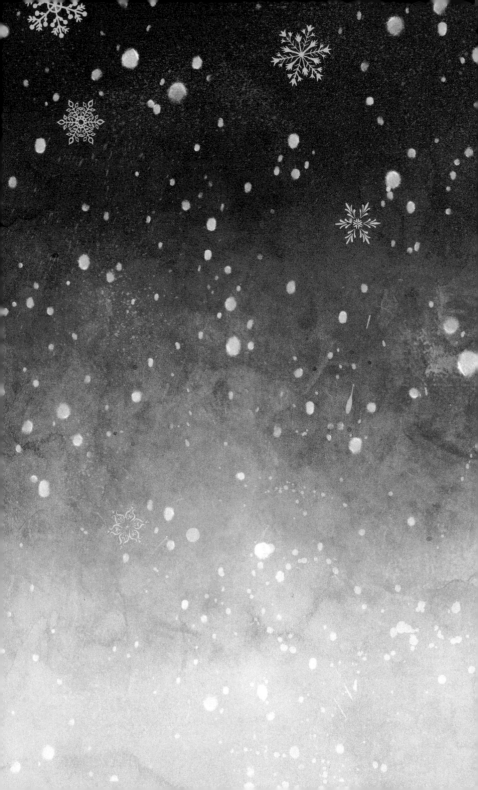

HER

 12

Like Chocolate

T wo AM text to Karou: *yawn stretch* Long day. Think I'll turn in now.

   Four seconds later: THAT'S NOT EVEN FUNNY

—Not even a little?

—TELL ME SOMETHING GOOD RIGHT NOW

—Let's see. Something good. *taps pencil against lip* Okay: ghost peacock

—???

—Used my 2nd-to-last scuppy to make peacock tracks appear in the snow.

— . . . of course. Um. Who wouldn't . . . ?

—And when Mik saw them, fireworks exploded in his brain. And then he kissed me.

—!!!!!!!!!!!!!!!!!!!!!!!!!!!!!kissing!!!!!!!!!!!!!!!!!!!!!!!!!!!!!!

I start to type a response, but I haven't gotten more than a couple of words in before the phone rings—as well it should, because this totally merits a phone call. I answer before the first ring is even finished. "So I'm totally going to make heart-shaped rock collections cool," I say. "Don't doubt that I can do it."

There's a pause, and then this voice that is not Karou's says, "That's uncanny, because I was just thinking of starting a blog that's all photos of my hands making heart shapes around different stuff. Like dog noses and funny graffiti." And the voice that is not Karou's is Mik's, and for a second I'm paralyzed, my brain kicking into damage-assessment mode, but I pretty much immediately realize that I'm lucky. Very lucky. There were a million more embarrassing things I might have said, and anyway: *Mik called me.* "And balloons stuck in trees," he says. "And ducklings in bathtubs."

"And clouds shaped like handguns," I contribute.

"*Yes.* And lewd root vegetables."

"And kids on leashes. And really bad clown makeup."

And it's like we talk on the phone in the middle of every night, it's that easy, and by the end of the call we're half-serious about the heart-hands blog, and, in spite of my efforts to hijack it in a misanthropic direction, it's a sweet idea, and Mik presses on undaunted with things like "baby feet" and "surprised ostriches," and I'm so *glad*.

"I should let you sleep," he says. "I just wanted to say good night."

"Good night," I say, sleepy, and happy with this layer-cake happiness that goes from bone-deep contentment—luxurious and almost lazy, like a hot bath—to fizzing, sparkler-in-the-heart-hole happiness that's waking up new parts of my brain and teaching them dance steps.

Mik says, "And I wanted to make sure you didn't

think, um, that I . . . hesitated . . . before because I didn't want to kiss you."

"No," I say, though I did think that—or fear it—for a few minutes in the rowboat. I get it now, though, and there's not a molecule in me that thinks that kiss was forced or reluctant or lukewarm. The kiss. The kiss spoke for itself. It erased all doubt. "It's okay. It couldn't be orchestrated. It had to just happen."

"I'm glad it did," he says.

"Me, too."

"Do you think . . . maybe it can happen again tomorrow? With dinner? No, I can't wait that long. Lunch? No. Breakfast?"

Oh, I guess so. I'm radiating lighthouse beams in my bedroom. "Yes please."

And we make plans and say good-bye, and I hang up. A few call-interrupts came while we were talking, and I didn't check them then but I see now that they were Karou, a voice mail and a string of texts, the last of which reads:

—Whyyyyyyyy are you torturing meeeeeeeee?
—Sorry! Sorry! Mik called.

And it hits me again. *Mik called me.* This is now a

thing that happens. And kissing. Kissing is going to be a regular part of my life now. I just see it, with this rare kind of clarity. It's an open horizon before us, as far as the eye can see: no angst and no games, just mutual delight. So simple, but so rich. Like chocolate. Not a gold-dusted truffle or a foofy pastry tower teetering on a crystal platter, but a plain, honest bar of the best chocolate in the world.

And I type a little more to Karou, and her happiness on my behalf practically wells out of the phone, but it's so late, and I really just want to lie on my bed and replay the night in my head, so I sign off with a promise to call her in the morning, and then I lie there remembering.

The sensation of falling, as Mik leaned down. His eyes were so near, and his lips, and I didn't know which to look at, his lips or his eyes, and then . . . I just. Eyes, up close. I've never. His eyes are blue, and blue eyes up close are a celestial phenomenon: nebulas as seen through telescopes, the light of unnamed stars diffused through dusts and elements and endlessness. Layers of light. Blue eyes are starlight. I never knew. His lashes fluttered shut before mine; I know because I have a strobe-quick memory of his eyelashes dusted with perfect lace-pattern snowflakes—and then darkness as my eyes closed, too, and all my awareness poured out into my other senses.

Touch. The softness of lips.

At first, okay, there wasn't so much softness as frozen-faced numbness, but really it just made me that much more aware of our breath, because our breath was warm and every second that our lips moved near and against each other in this feather-light way, I could *feel* more. It was like something coming into focus. I couldn't say at what point I could feel fully, just that we got there. We got there slowly and exquisitely, our breath touching more than our actual lips, so that each small brush of contact was wrapped in longing for the next, and I learned this: The eye's perception of texture is pale compared to the lips', and I didn't know what velvety was until I knew it with my lips.

Oh, kissing. Oh, violin boy.

I'm not sure how long it was. I couldn't begin to guess. Somewhere between two minutes and twenty, and while it never stopped being *sweet*, it did, toward the end, start hinting at the mysterious connectivity of nerves, little rivers of fire that zither through your entire body awakening sleeper cells of feeling, each one adding another dimension to this mysterious inner landscape that is so much bigger than it seems, possibly infinitely, unknowably bigger. And reflexology no longer seems like hokum to me, because if a light touch at the nape of my neck can do *that* to my knees, then, where the human body is concerned . . . anything might be possible.

My knees were what finally called time-out on the kiss, because they started to tremble and Mik thought I was shivering, but I totally wasn't, and the way we looked at each other after the kiss was breathless and a little bit startled—oh *hi*—and unself-consciously happy, and dazzled, and thoroughly, deeply, mutually ensorcelled.

So, you know, that was nice.

My phone again, just as I'm drifting off to sleep. A text. It's Karou: **Have to know. If ghost peacock was 2nd-to-last scuppy, what did you do with the LAST?**

And my hand goes to it—no longer hidden in a coat pocket but hanging from a long silver chain around my neck: a singular red bead. I didn't need it. Well, I didn't need any of them, but I'm glad I had them, because they inspired me to create this night—right up to the point when the night took over, with Mik's help, and started to create itself. Which is what one always hopes will happen: for life to take over and be bigger and more marvelous than what we can dream up on our own.

Life doesn't need magic to be magical.

(But a little bit sure doesn't hurt.)

It's nice knowing I have this one last scuppy if I ever need to whip up some peacock footprints—literal or figurative—but maybe I'll just end up keeping it as a souvenir. Who knows? **Saving it for a rainy day,** I text back to Karou, and I cup the bead in my hand and smile as I drift toward sleep, wondering what my rainy days are going to look like now. As good as my snowy ones, I think.

I'm going to need a bigger umbrella.

With my dear Karou (we are so fierce!)

One remains! (decisions, decisions...)

Zuzana's sketchbook of genius

ACKNOWLEDGMENTS

This little book was such a joy to write, like eating macarons between courses in the big, fraught worlds-spanning saga of Daughter of Smoke & Bone. Thank God for Mik and Zuzana! I owe them such a debt for keeping the darkness at bay throughout the series. I could always count on them for some kissing and laughter when it was most needed, and I'm so happy that this story gets to be an object in the world now, after existing only in the ethereal realms (aka e-readers) for the past few years.

Thank you to Little, Brown Books for Young Readers for making that happen! Thank you to Alvina for deciding it was time, and for wanting it to be as special and magical as possible. Thanks to the whole amazing team: Megan Tingley, Jackie Engel, Emilie Polster, Jen

Graham, Lisa Moraleda, Nikki Garcia, Jane Lee, Jennifer McClelland-Smith, Carol Scatorchio, Shawn Foster, Karina Granda, and Sasha Illingworth. The whole process has been a joy.

Giant thanks to Jane Putch for shepherding this book through its various incarnations. You're the best.

And thank you most of all to Jim Di Bartolo for making it look like this!!! I love it so much! You brought the perfect mix of humor and beauty, and have created a reading experience that spills off the page so that we feel like we're holding the story's artifacts in our hands. It's perfect. And thank you, too, for inspiring my romantical-type thoughts all these years and helping me thoroughly research kissing and stuff so that I can write about it as well as possible. (The things we do for art!) I love you.

—*Laini Taylor*

My additional grateful thanks to the entire art and production team at Little, Brown, specifically Karina Granda, Nikki Garcia, and Sasha Illingworth for their design guidance and care, and of course Alvina Ling for making this and so many gorgeous books become a reality. Thank you for considering the gas mask!

To Jane Putch, for her constant friendship, support, and enthusiasm—you're a treasure and a gift!

May everyone wanting love and romance in their lives (and isn't that everyone?) get to spend their days with the perfectly matching puzzle piece to their heart.

To our daughter, Clementine. May you find a kind, creative, happy person to win your heart someday...like your mother, Laini, won mine years ago.

And most importantly, for Laini, my constant muse and ideal life partner. Thank you for creating such an imaginative world for Zuzana and Mik to occupy and for giving that world so much heart. You make every day a unique treat, and an unending reminder of love and magic: Thank the stars for you!

—*Jim Di Bartolo*

Turn the page for a
graphic-novel adaptation of a scene from
DAUGHTER OF SMOKE & BONE, from
New York Times bestselling author Laini Taylor,
illustrated by Jim Di Bartolo.

Oh, good.
Pestilence is free.

Sometimes Karou's errands took a few hours; other times, she was gone for days and returned weary and disheveled, maybe pale, maybe sunburned, or with a limp --

-- or possibly a bite mark...

...and once with an unshakable fever that had turned out to be malaria.

Just where did you happen to pick up a tropical disease?

On the tram, maybe? This old woman did sneeze right in my face the other day.

That is not how you get malaria.

I know. It was gross, though. I'm thinking of getting a moped so I don't have to take the tram anymore.

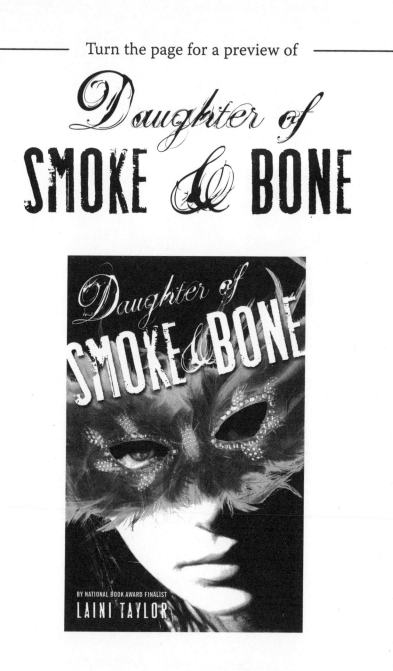

Once upon a time,
an angel and a devil fell in love.

It did not end well.

❧ 1 ❧

Impossible to Scare

Walking to school over the snow-muffled cobbles, Karou had no sinister premonitions about the day. It seemed like just another Monday, innocent but for its essential Mondayness, not to mention its Januaryness. It was cold, and it was dark— in the dead of winter the sun didn't rise until eight—but it was also lovely. The falling snow and the early hour conspired to paint Prague ghostly, like a tintype photograph, all silver and haze.

On the riverfront thoroughfare, trams and buses roared past, grounding the day in the twenty-first century, but on the quieter lanes, the wintry peace might have hailed from another time. Snow and stone and ghostlight, Karou's own footsteps and the feather of steam from her coffee mug, and she was alone and adrift in mundane thoughts: school, errands. The occasional cheek-chew of bitterness when a pang of heartache intruded, as pangs of heartache will, but she pushed them aside, resolute, ready to be done with all that.

She held her coffee mug in one hand and clutched her coat closed with the other. An artist's portfolio was slung over her shoulder, and her hair — loose, long, and peacock blue — was gathering a lace of snowflakes.

Just another day.

And then.

A snarl, rushing footfall, and she was seized from behind, pulled hard against a man's broad chest as hands yanked her scarf askew and she felt teeth — *teeth* — against her neck.

Nibbling.

Her attacker was *nibbling* her.

Annoyed, she tried to shake him off without spilling her coffee, but some sloshed out of her cup anyway, into the dirty snow.

"Jesus, Kaz, get off," she snapped, spinning to face her ex-boyfriend. The lamplight was soft on his beautiful face. *Stupid beauty*, she thought, shoving him away. *Stupid face.*

"How did you know it was me?" he asked.

"It's always you. And it never works."

Kazimir made his living jumping out from behind things, and it frustrated him that he could never get even the slightest rise out of Karou. "You're impossible to scare," he complained, giving her the pout he thought was irresistible. Until recently, she wouldn't have resisted it. She would have risen on tiptoe and licked his pout-puckered lower lip, licked it languorously and then taken it between her teeth and teased it before losing herself in a kiss that made her melt against him like sun-warmed honey.

Those days were so over.

"Maybe you're just not scary," she said, and walked on.

Kaz caught up and strolled at her side, hands in pockets. "I *am* scary, though. The snarl? The bite? Anyone normal would have a heart attack. Just not you, ice water for blood."

When she ignored him, he added, "Josef and I are starting a new tour. Old Town *vampire* tour. The tourists will eat it up."

They would, thought Karou. They paid good money for Kaz's "ghost tours," which consisted of being herded through the tangled lanes of Prague in the dark, pausing at sites of supposed murders so "ghosts" could leap out of doorways and make them shriek. She'd played a ghost herself on several occasions, had held aloft a bloody head and moaned while the tourists' screams gave way to laughter. It had been fun.

Kaz had been fun. Not anymore. "Good luck with that," she said, staring ahead, her voice colorless.

"We could use you," Kaz said.

"No."

"You could play a sexy vampire vixen —"

"No."

"Lure in the men —"

"No."

"You could wear your cape...."

Karou stiffened.

Softly, Kaz coaxed, "You still have it, don't you, baby? Most beautiful thing I've ever seen, you with that black silk against your white skin —"

"Shut up," she hissed, coming to a halt in the middle of Maltese Square. *God*, she thought. How stupid had she been to fall for this petty, pretty street actor, dress up for him and give him memories like that? Exquisitely stupid.

Lonely stupid.

Kaz lifted his hand to brush a snowflake from her eyelashes. She said, "Touch me and you'll get this coffee in your face."

He lowered his hand. "Roo, Roo, my fierce Karou. When will you stop fighting me? I said I was sorry."

"Be sorry, then. Just be sorry somewhere else." They spoke in Czech, and her acquired accent matched his native one perfectly.

He sighed, irritated that Karou was still resisting his apologies. This wasn't in his script. "Come on," he coaxed. His voice was rough and soft at the same time, like a blues singer's mix of gravel and silk. "We're meant to be together, you and me."

Meant. Karou sincerely hoped that if she were "meant" for anyone, it wasn't Kaz. She looked at him, beautiful Kazimir whose smile used to work on her like a summons, compelling her to his side. And that had seemed a glorious place to be, as if colors were brighter there, sensations more profound. It had also, she'd discovered, been a *popular* place, other girls occupying it when she did not.

"Get Svetla to be your vampire vixen," she said. "She's got the vixen part down."

He looked pained. "I don't want Svetla. I want you."

"Alas. I am not an option."

"Don't say that," he said, reaching for her hand.

She pulled back, a pang of heartache surging in spite of all her efforts at aloofness. *Not worth it,* she told herself. *Not even close.* "This is the definition of stalking, you realize."

"Puh. I'm not stalking you. I happen to be going this way."

"Right," said Karou. They were just a few doors from her

school now. The Art Lyceum of Bohemia was a private high school housed in a pink Baroque palace where famously, during the Nazi occupation, two young Czech nationalists had slit the throat of a Gestapo commander and scrawled *liberty* with his blood. A brief, brave rebellion before they were captured and impaled upon the finials of the courtyard gate. Now students were milling around that very gate, smoking, waiting for friends. But Kaz wasn't a student—at twenty, he was several years older than Karou—and she had never known him to be out of bed before noon. "Why are you even awake?"

"I have a new job," he said. "It starts early."

"What, you're doing *morning* vampire tours?"

"Not that. Something else. An...*unveiling* of sorts." He was grinning now. Gloating. He wanted her to ask what his new job was.

She wouldn't ask. With perfect disinterest she said, "Well, have fun with that," and walked away.

Kaz called after her, "Don't you want to know what it is?" The grin was still there. She could hear it in his voice.

"Don't care," she called back, and went through the gate.

* * *

She really should have asked.

❦ 2 ❦

An Unveiling of Sorts

Monday, Wednesday, and Friday, Karou's first class was life drawing. When she walked into the studio, her friend Zuzana was already there and had staked out easels for them in front of the model's platform. Karou shrugged off her portfolio and coat, unwound her scarf, and announced, "I'm being stalked."

Zuzana arched an eyebrow. She was a master of the eyebrow arch, and Karou envied her for it. Her own eyebrows did not function independently of each other, which handicapped her expressions of suspicion and disdain.

Zuzana could do both perfectly, but this was milder eyebrow action, mere cool curiosity. "Don't tell me Jackass tried to scare you again."

"He's going through a vampire phase. He bit my neck."

"Actors," muttered Zuzana. "I'm telling you, you need to tase the loser. Teach him to go jumping out at people."

"I don't have a Taser." Karou didn't add that she didn't need a Taser; she was more than capable of defending herself without electricity. She'd had an unusual education.

"Well, get one. Seriously. Bad behavior should be punished. Plus, it would be fun. Don't you think? I've always wanted to tase someone. *Zap!*" Zuzana mimicked convulsions.

Karou shook her head. "No, tiny violent one, I don't think it would be fun. You're terrible."

"I am not terrible. Kaz is terrible. Tell me I don't have to remind you." She gave Karou a sharp look. "Tell me you're not even considering forgiving him."

"*No,*" declared Karou. "But try getting *him* to believe that." Kaz just couldn't fathom any girl willfully depriving herself of his charms. And what had she done but strengthen his vanity those months they'd been together, gazing at him starry-eyed, giving him...everything? His wooing her now, she thought, was a point of pride, to prove to himself that he could have who he wanted. That it was up to him.

Maybe Zuzana was right. Maybe she *should* tase him.

"Sketchbook," commanded Zuzana, holding out her hand like a surgeon for a scalpel.

Karou's best friend was bossy in obverse proportion to her size. She only passed five feet in her platform boots, whereas Karou was five foot six but seemed taller in the same way that ballerinas do, with their long necks and willowy limbs. She wasn't a ballerina, but she had the look, in figure if not in fashion. Not many ballerinas have bright blue hair or a constellation of tattoos on their limbs, and Karou had both.

The only tattoos visible as she dug out her sketchbook and handed it over were the ones on her wrists like bracelets—a single word on each: *true* and *story*.

As Zuzana took the book, a couple of other students, Pavel and Dina, crowded in to look over her shoulder. Karou's sketchbooks had a cult following around school and were handed around and marveled at on a daily basis. This one—number ninety-two in a lifelong series—was bound with rubber bands, and as soon as Zuzana took them off it burst open, each page so coated in gesso and paint that the binding could scarcely contain them. As it fanned open, Karou's trademark characters wavered on the pages, gorgeously rendered and deeply strange.

There was Issa, serpent from the waist down and woman from the waist up, with the bare, globe breasts of Kama Sutra carvings, the hood and fangs of a cobra, and the face of an angel.

Giraffe-necked Twiga, hunched over with his jeweler's glass stuck in one squinting eye.

Yasri, parrot-beaked and human-eyed, a frill of orange curls escaping her kerchief. She was carrying a platter of fruit and a pitcher of wine.

And Brimstone, of course—he was the star of the sketchbooks. Here he was shown with Kishmish perched on the curl of one of his great ram's horns. In the fantastical stories Karou told in her sketchbooks, Brimstone dealt in wishes. Sometimes she called him the Wishmonger; other times, simply "the grump."

She'd been drawing these creatures since she was a little girl, and her friends tended to talk about them as if they were real. "What was Brimstone up to this weekend?" asked Zuzana.

"The usual," said Karou. "Buying teeth from murderers. He got some Nile crocodile teeth yesterday from this awful Somali poacher, but the idiot tried to steal from him and got half strangled by his snake collar. He's lucky to be alive."

Zuzana found the story illustrated on the book's last drawn pages: the Somali, his eyes rolling back in his head as the whip-thin snake around his neck cinched itself as tight as a garrote. Humans, Karou had explained before, had to submit to wearing one of Issa's serpents around their necks before they could enter Brimstone's shop. That way if they tried anything fishy they were easy to subdue—by strangulation, which wasn't always fatal, or, if necessary, by a bite to the throat, which was.

"How do you make this stuff up, maniac?" Zuzana asked, all jealous wonderment.

"Who says I do? I keep telling you, it's all real."

"Uh-huh. And your hair grows out of your head that color, too."

"What? It totally does," said Karou, passing a long blue strand through her fingers.

"Right."

Karou shrugged and gathered her hair back in a messy coil, stabbing a paintbrush through it to secure it at the nape of her neck. In fact, her hair did grow out of her head that color, pure as ultramarine straight from the paint tube, but that was a truth she told with a certain wry smile, as if she were being absurd. Over the years she'd found that that was all it took, that lazy smile, and she could tell the truth without risk of being believed. It was easier than keeping track of lies, and so it became part of who she was: Karou with her wry smile and crazy imagination.

In fact, it was not her imagination that was crazy. It was her life — blue hair and Brimstone and all.

Zuzana handed the book to Pavel and started flipping pages in her own oversize drawing pad, searching for a fresh page. "I wonder who's posing today."

"Probably Wiktor," said Karou. "We haven't had him in a while."

"I know. I'm hoping he's dead."

"Zuzana!"

"What? He's eight million years old. We might as well draw the anatomical skeleton as that creepy bonesack."

There were some dozen models, male and female, all shapes and ages, who rotated through the class. They ranged from enormous Madame Svobodnik, whose flesh was more landscape than figure, to pixie Eliska with her wasp waist, the favorite of the male students. Ancient Wiktor was Zuzana's least favorite. She claimed to have nightmares whenever she had to draw him.

"He looks like an unwrapped mummy." She shuddered. "I ask you, is staring at a naked old man any way to start the day?"

"Better than getting attacked by a vampire," said Karou.

In fact, she didn't mind drawing Wiktor. For one thing, he was so nearsighted he never made eye contact with the students, which was a bonus. No matter that she had been drawing nudes for years; she still found it unsettling, sketching one of the younger male models, to look up from a study of his penis — a necessary study; you couldn't exactly leave the area blank — and find him staring back at her. Karou had felt her cheeks flame on plenty of occasions and ducked behind her easel.

Those occasions, as it turned out, were about to fade into insignificance next to the mortification of today.

She was sharpening a pencil with a razor blade when Zuzana blurted in a weird, choked voice, "Oh my god, Karou!"

And before she even looked up, she knew.

An *unveiling*, he had said. Oh, how clever. She lifted her gaze from her pencil and took in the sight of Kaz standing beside Profesorka Fiala. He was barefoot and wearing a robe, and his shoulder-length golden hair, which had minutes before been wind-teased and sparkling with snowflakes, was pulled back in a ponytail. His face was a perfect blend of Slavic angles and soft sensuality: cheekbones that might have been turned on a diamond cutter's lathe, lips you wanted to touch with your fingertips to see if they felt like velvet. Which, Karou knew, they did. Stupid lips.

Murmurs went around the room. *A new model, oh my god, gorgeous . . .*

One murmur cut through the others: "Isn't that Karou's boyfriend?"

Ex, she wanted to snap. So very, very *ex*.

"I think it is. *Look* at him. . . ."

Karou *was* looking at him, her face frozen in what she hoped was a mask of impervious calm. *Don't blush*, she commanded herself. *Do not blush.* Kaz looked right back at her, a smile dimpling one cheek, eyes lazy and amused. And when he was sure he held her gaze, he had the nerve to wink.

A flurry of giggles erupted around Karou.

"Oh, the evil bastard . . ." Zuzana breathed.

Kaz stepped up onto the model's platform. He looked straight at Karou as he untied his sash; he looked at her as he shrugged off the robe. And then Karou's ex-boyfriend was standing before her entire class, beautiful as heartbreak, naked as the *David*. And on his chest, right over his heart, was a new tattoo.

It was an elaborate cursive K.

More giggles burst forth. Students didn't know who to look at, Karou or Kazimir, and glanced from one to the other, waiting for a drama to unfold. "Quiet!" commanded Profesorka Fiala, appalled, clapping her hands together until the laughter was stifled. Karou's blush came on then. She couldn't stop it. First her chest and neck went hot, then her face. Kaz's eyes were on her the whole time, and his dimple deepened with satisfaction when he saw her flustered.

"One-minute poses, please, Kazimir," said Fiala.

Kaz stepped into his first pose. It was dynamic, as the one-minute poses were meant to be — twisted torso, taut muscles, limbs stretched in simulation of action. These warm-up sketches were all about movement and loose line, and Kaz was taking the opportunity to flaunt himself. Karou thought she didn't hear a lot of pencils scratching. Were the other girls in the class just staring stupidly, as she was?

She dipped her head, took up her sharp pencil — thinking of other uses she would happily put it to — and started to sketch. Quick, fluid lines, and all the sketches on one page; she overlapped them so they looked like an illustration of dance.

Kaz was graceful. He spent enough time looking in the mirror that he knew how to use his body for effect. It was his instrument, he'd have said. Along with the voice, the body was an actor's tool. Well, Kaz was a lousy actor — which was why he got by on ghost tours and the occasional low-budget production of *Faust*—but he made a fine artist's model, as Karou knew, having drawn him many times before.

His body had reminded Karou, from the first time she saw it...unveiled...of a Michelangelo. Unlike some Renaissance artists, who'd favored slim, effete models, Michelangelo had gone for power, drawing broad-shouldered quarry workers and somehow managing to render them both carnal and elegant at the same time. That was Kaz: carnal and elegant.

And deceitful. And narcissistic. And, honestly, kind of dumb.

"Karou!" The British girl Helen was whispering harshly, trying to get her attention. "Is that him?"

Karou didn't acknowledge her. She drew, pretending everything was normal. Just another day in class. And if the model had an insolent dimple and wouldn't take his eyes off her? She ignored it as best she could.

When the timer rang, Kaz calmly gathered up his robe and put it on. Karou hoped it wouldn't occur to him that he was free to walk around the studio. *Stay where you are,* she willed him. But he didn't. He sauntered toward her.

"Hi, Jackass," said Zuzana. "Modest much?"

Ignoring her, he asked Karou, "Like my new tattoo?"

Students were standing up to stretch, but rather than dispersing for smoke or bathroom breaks, they hovered casually within earshot.

"Sure," Karou said, keeping her voice light. "K for *Kazimir*, right?"

"Funny girl. You know what it's for."

"Well," she mused in Thinker pose, "I know there's only one

person you really love, and his name does start with a K. But I can think of a better place for it than your heart." She took up her pencil and, on her last drawing of Kaz, inscribed a K right over his classically sculpted buttock.

Zuzana laughed, and Kaz's jaw tightened. Like most vain people, he hated to be mocked. "I'm not the only one with a tattoo, am I, Karou?" he asked. He looked to Zuzana. "Has she shown it to you?"

Zuzana gave Karou the suspicious rendition of the eyebrow arch.

"I don't know which you mean," Karou lied calmly. "I have lots of tattoos." To demonstrate, she didn't flash *true* or *story*, or the serpent coiled around her ankle, or any of her other concealed works of art. Rather, she held up her hands in front of her face, palms out. In the center of each was an eye inked in deepest indigo, in effect turning her hands into hamsas, those ancient symbols of warding against the evil eye. Palm tattoos are notorious for fading, but Karou's never did. She'd had these eyes as long as she could remember; for all she knew of their origin, she could have been born with them.

"Not those," said Kaz. "I mean the one that says *Kazimir*, right over your heart."

"I don't have a tattoo like that." She made herself sound puzzled and unfastened the top few buttons of her sweater. Beneath was a camisole, and she lowered it by a few revealing inches to demonstrate that indeed there was no tattoo above her breast. The skin there was white as milk.

Kaz blinked. "What? How did you—?"

"Come with me." Zuzana grabbed Karou's hand and pulled

her away. As they wove among the easels, all eyes were on Karou, lit with curiosity.

"Karou, did you break up?" Helen whispered in English, but Zuzana put up her hand in an imperious gesture that silenced her, and she dragged Karou out of the studio and into the girls' bathroom. There, eyebrow still arched, she asked, "What the hell was that?"

"What?"

"*What?* You practically flashed the boy."

"Please. I did not flash him."

"Whatever. What's this about a tattoo over your heart?"

"I just showed you. There's nothing there." She saw no reason to add that there *had* been something; she preferred to pretend she had never been so stupid. Plus, explaining how she'd gotten rid of it was not exactly an option.

"Well, good. The last thing you need is that idiot's name on your body. Can you believe him? Does he think if he just dangles his boy bits at you like a cat toy you'll go scampering after him?"

"Of course he thinks that," said Karou. "This is his idea of a romantic gesture."

"All you have to do is tell Fiala he's a stalker, and she'll throw his ass out."

Karou had thought of that, but she shook her head. Surely she could come up with a better way to get Kaz out of her class and out of her life. She had means at her disposal that most people didn't. She'd think of something.

"The boy is not terrible to draw, though." Zuzana went to the mirror and flipped wisps of dark hair across her forehead. "Got to give him that."

"Yeah. Too bad he's such a gargantuan asshole."

"A giant, stupid orifice," Zuzana agreed.

"A walking, talking cranny."

"Cranny." Zuzana laughed. "I like."

An idea came to Karou, and a faintly villainous smirk crossed her face.

"What?" asked Zuzana, seeing it.

"Nothing. We'd better get back in there."

"You're sure? You don't have to."

Karou nodded. "Nothing to it."

Kaz had gotten all the satisfaction he was going to get from this cute little ploy of his. It was her turn now. Walking back into the studio, she reached up and touched the necklace she was wearing, a multistrand loop of African trade beads in every color. At least they looked like African trade beads. They were more than that. Not much more, but enough for what Karou had planned.

About the Author and Illustrator

New York Times bestselling author and National Book Award finalist **Laini Taylor**'s works include *Strange the Dreamer* and the Daughter of Smoke & Bone trilogy: *Daughter of Smoke & Bone, Days of Blood & Starlight, Dreams of Gods & Monsters*, and now this illustrated companion, *Night of Cake & Puppets*. She is also the author of *Lips Touch: Three Times* and the Dreamdark books: *Blackbringer* and *Silksinger*. Her website is lainitaylor.com.

Jim Di Bartolo is a mixed-media illustrator, painter, visual storyteller, and writer. In his freelance career he has illustrated novels, comic books, and role-playing games and painted private commissions. Some of his works include *In the Shadows* (coauthored with Kiersten White) and the collaborative novel with his wife, Laini Taylor, *Lips Touch: Three Times*, which was a National Book Award finalist. His website is jimdibartolo.com.

Laini and Jim live in Portland, Oregon, with their daughter, Clementine.